Sending The Staff Home To Leave Himself Alone In The Castle With A Female Guest Had The Makings Of A Classic Seduction.

Jennifer wasn't sure if she was nervous or excited as Christopher led her upstairs. But she was out of breath by the time they reached the top.

"Is something wrong, Jennifer?" The earl's eyes narrowed with suspicion. "If I'd wanted to attack you, don't you think I would have done it before now?"

"Oh no, I wasn't thinking—"

"Yes, you were. You've read too many gothic novels, luv. Here—"

Before she could pull away, his lips settled tenderly over hers. It was over as quickly as it had begun. "What was that for?" she gasped.

"To prove I could kiss you without being driven mad by passion."

"I see." As to her own passion or sanity, Jennifer couldn't presently vouch for either. Because with his arms enclosing her, she felt as near to heaven as she'd ever been.

Dear Reader,

Happy New Year from Silhouette Desire, where we offer you six passionate, powerful and provocative romances every month of the year! Here's what you can indulge yourself with this January....

Begin the new year with a seductive MAN OF THE MONTH, *Tall, Dark & Western* by Anne Marie Winston. A rancher seeking a marriage of convenience places a personals ad for a wife, only to fall—hard—for the single mom who responds!

Silhouette Desire proudly presents a sequel to the wildly successful in-line continuity series THE TEXAS CATTLEMAN'S CLUB. This exciting *new* series about alpha men on a mission is called TEXAS CATTLEMAN'S CLUB: LONE STAR JEWELS. Jennifer Greene's launch book, *Millionaire M.D.*, features a wealthy surgeon who helps out his childhood crush when she finds a baby on her doorstep—by marrying her!

Alexandra Sellers continues her exotic miniseries SONS OF THE DESERT with one more irresistible sheikh in *Sheikh's Woman*. THE BARONS OF TEXAS miniseries by Fayrene Preston returns with another feisty Baron heroine in *The Barons of Texas: Kit*. In Kathryn Jensen's *The Earl's Secret*, a British aristocrat romances a U.S. commoner while wrestling with a secret. And Shirley Rogers offers *A Cowboy, a Bride & a Wedding Vow*, in which a cowboy discovers his secret child.

So ring in the new year with lots of cheer and plenty of red-hot romance, by reading all six of these enticing love stories.

Enjoy!

Joan Marlow Golan

Joan Marlow Golan
Senior Editor, Silhouette Desire

Please address questions and book requests to:
Silhouette Reader Service
U.S.: 3010 Walden Ave., P.O. Box 1325, Buffalo, NY 14269
Canadian: P.O. Box 609, Fort Erie, Ont. L2A 5X3

Books by Kathryn Jensen

Silhouette Desire

I Married a Prince #1115
The Earl Takes a Bride #1282
Mail-Order Cinderella #1318
The Earl's Secret #1343

Silhouette Intimate Moments

Time and Again #685
Angel's Child #758
The Twelve-Month Marriage #797

KATHRYN JENSEN

has written many novels for young readers as well as for adults. She speed walks, works out with weights and enjoys ballroom dancing for exercise, stress reduction and pleasure. Her children are now grown. She lives in Maryland with her writing companion—Sunny, a lovable terrier mix adopted from a shelter.

Having worked as a hospital switchboard operator, department store sales associate, bank clerk and elementary school teacher, she now splits her days between writing her own books and teaching fiction writing at two local colleges and through a correspondence course. She enjoys helping new writers get a start, and speaks "at the drop of a hat" at writers' conferences, libraries and schools across the country.

One

Life had taken a wrong turn somewhere. And no matter how hard the young earl of Winchester tried, he couldn't seem to put it right.

At the top of the castle's north turret was his favorite room, his refuge and place to be alone with his most private thoughts. As a small child he and his brothers had played here. All through adolescent summers, this was where he came to read of valiant knights, courageous battles and beautiful yet desperate princesses. He was always victorious in his daydreams, and he had been comforted when his young spirit was troubled.

But these adult days, when he spent time within the thick granite walls, the thoughts that curled round him like the mists off Loch Kerr only blackened his already dark mood. His frustration and anger grew day by day, gathering power like a storm rolling across the Scottish moor, until he came perilously close to lashing out at anything or anyone who crossed him.

Stepping out onto the stone balcony, Christopher Smythe glowered across the fragrant purple heather. Three hundred miles to the south lay London, where most of his elite circle of friends would spend a few days before drifting en masse for the month of August to the Côte d'Azur. His houseguests were frequent and usually an effective distraction, but eventually they left for a new foxhunt, the next polo match or house party. Then he had no choice but to face his helpless fury, because he was unable to act on man's deepest instinct.

Christopher's strong hands gripped the stone balustrade as he lifted his face to the morning sky and loudly cursed it and fate, too. Instead of feeling better for unleashing his rage, he experienced something else. An almost overwhelming sense that his life was about to become still more complicated before he could hope for peace of mind.

It was then that he thought he saw something move at the distant end of the narrow gravel drive leading up the hill from the main road. It appeared to be a van of sorts: red, squat and dusty. His housekeeper didn't drive, and his caretaker was off for the day. The stable master and his lads were busy tending to his horses. He wasn't expecting the stone mason's crew to return for another few days. In fact, no one he knew drove a boxy little vehicle like that.

As the crimson monstrosity rumbled closer, kicking up dust and pebbles like a skittish mare, he squinted at a brightly colored magnetic sign attached to one side: Murphy's Worldwide Escapes. A lost party of tourists, he thought grimly. There was nothing to do now but go down and give them directions back to the highway.

Irritated that his brooding had been interrupted—or because the interruption promised to be so brief and unexciting—he hurried down the turret's tight coil of steps to the landing. In long, purposeful strides he took another flight, two ivory marble steps at a time to the great hall on the ground level. Christopher flung open the weighty, iron-nubbed oak door and stepped outside to see a young woman climb down from the driver's seat of the van and cheerfully wave her passengers out onto his property.

This was too much.

"What the bloody hell do you think you're doing?" He rushed at her, feeling heat rise up from his collar and settle like a steaming blanket over his face.

She spun around, staring at him, lips parted in surprise. Her eyes were the color of new leaves. Fresh, green, virginal. They darkened the instant they settled upon his scowl. "Excuse me?"

"Didn't you see *the sign?*"

"What sign?" There was a note of challenge in her voice, which surprised him. Usually he was able to send intruders scurrying with a simple glare.

"The one that says this is private property," he growled. "'No Trespassing.'"

She blinked at him twice, nibbled at her lower lip and sighed. "Well, I guess I just assumed we weren't..." Peering into her purse, she rummaged around inside. "Here it is." She shook a piece of paper in his face. "We have reservations for 11:00 a.m."

"Reservations?" He snapped the paper from between her fingers and unfolded it.

It seemed to be some sort of confirmation letter, indicating that her party had arrangements to tour Bremerley Castle. He opened his mouth to inform her Bremerley was a good twenty kilometers to the north along the coast, nearly as far as Edinburgh. But he could see her customers were looking expectantly up at the castle walls, and behind her brave front those green eyes appeared worried.

The outer layers of his anger sloughed away: he felt his brow cool, the tense muscles of his shoulders settle. He didn't have the heart to tell her in front of the others that she was as lost as a little mole out of its hole.

Besides, she looked adorable, standing there in front of him, running her tongue over her upper lip and gazing up at him with those lovely pale-green eyes. A sudden, inexplicable finger of lust poked at his insides.

"I'll be happy to show you around," he growled with as good a nature as any bear woken from hibernation.

Her expression immediately brightened. "Oh, good. You must be the caretaker. Is Lord MacKinney in residence this time of year?"

The unexpected chance of a game pleased him, almost to the point of bringing a smile to his lips. Why not pretend to be someone else for just a little while? And if it helped out this misplaced but lovely young American—so much the better. "Occasionally," he said. "When he isn't off playing polo or attending theater in London. He's not here today."

She winked at him conspiratorially. "You're probably happy to have him out from underfoot."

He bent down close to her ear and caught a whiff

of vanilla-scented perfume. "Oh, he can be quite a handful, he can."

"Well then, I'm glad he's not around." She turned to admire the soaring stone fortress, her eyes wide, sparkling and delightfully childlike. "Will you show us the rooms that are open to the public?"

The long curve of her throat drew his attention, summoning a momentary vision of his lips trailing down the delicate flesh, that lust finger poking him again. She was petite—a natural blonde, he guessed, though that wasn't a sure thing these days. She stood only as high as his shoulder, even in her conservative heels. As she studied the structure that had belonged to his family for nearly three hundred years, her fingers played lightly with the tassels at the bottom of her tapestry purse. A momentary frown puckered her brow, and she looked with more concentration at the right wing, which remained in ruins.

Clever woman, he thought. Bremerley had been fully restored, and if she were a competent guide, she would know that. He wondered how long it would take her to figure out her mistake.

Meanwhile he took pleasure in her interest in his legacy. Usually, when tourists took a wrong turn off the A7 and ended up on his grounds, he or his groundskeeper brusquely sent them on their way. But she was so damn fascinating to watch.

"What is your name?" he asked, gesturing with one hand toward the steps.

She started walking, and her group of ten chattering travelers followed their shepherdess like docile lambs. "Jennifer Murphy, and you?"

"Christopher."

"Christopher," she repeated thoughtfully as she

climbed the granite stairs, worn low and smooth in
their centers by past generations. "Is that a Scottish
name? I would have thought English. As in Christopher Robin."

"I was born in Sussex. I grew up in that area, and
in London."

"How exciting!" Her eyes danced in the morning
light.

"Sometimes," he admitted. He certainly hadn't
fretted about where his next meal was coming from,
and there had always been plenty of money with
which to do anything he liked. His father, the earl of
Sussex, had been grudging with his affection, but he'd
placidly doled out cash to Christopher and his two
brothers whenever required, as well as titles. They
each could legitimately claim to be an earl—although
of lesser importance than their father. The family held
a collection of aristocratic nametags dating back centuries, gathered from various ancestors on their father's side.

"What about you? You're obviously an American.
What part of the States are you from?"

"I grew up in Baltimore, and I've lived there all
of my life. My mother and I own a travel agency. We
specialize in European tours."

"And you personally guide each tour?"

She smiled. "Not every one. Most, though, since
my mother prefers to keep watch over the office. And
since I majored in history in college, I have the background for the on-site lectures we offer."

"Is that so?" Not only was she pretty, she was
smart, too. He itched to find out more about her. But
by now they were standing in the middle of the great

hall, and her group was getting restless and starting to investigate.

He was about to ask her to warn her clients not to touch the paintings he'd just moved out of storage and propped against one stone wall to await hanging. But she was staring at his clothing, a frown softly rumpling her forehead. "Is something wrong?"

"I was just curious how much caretakers are paid these days." She flicked a finger at the lapel of his favorite cashmere blazer.

She was catching on fast. Christopher nearly chuckled.

He had dressed to drive into Edinburgh for a meeting with his solicitor. That was the way he and his father communicated these days. The old earl disapproved of his youngest son's lifestyle—as recorded in elaborate detail by the British paparazzi. His father considered him a playboy with a weakness for fast polo ponies and faster women. When Christopher had asked a year ago to be given Castle Donan as part of his inheritance, he had agreed in the hope Christopher would settle down in the North Country and find himself a bride. But he had been living at Donan for over nine months and that hadn't happened.

In actuality, the young earl thought to himself, he had only *one* weakness—which would remain a secret until the moment he was released from his promise. He hoped with all his heart that day would come soon.

Christopher forced a smile for the young woman's benefit. "The jacket is a gift from my employer."

Jennifer studied him for a moment longer through narrowed eyes, paling almost to buttercup-yellow. He wished he could tell what she was thinking. Suddenly she spun around and, with a quick clap of her hands above her head, summoned her group and began talking about the architecture of the Middle Ages. He listened to her, enthralled more by the sound of her words than by their meaning. Her voice was gentle and sweet, reminding him of a time in his distant past when a nanny, whose name he couldn't recall, had read him to sleep with stories of a time when honor meant everything.

He tried to imagine how Jennifer might look dressed in the garb of a fifteenth-century noblewoman. Today she wore a simple denim skirt and a pink cotton top. Back then it would have been a sweeping gown of Flemish damask, ribbons and jewels woven through her long, flaxen hair. Back then a man could legally shut away his woman behind stone walls, safe from the wandering eyes and lustful urges of other men.

Politically incorrect for the modern world, true… but the male fantasy intrigued him nonetheless. He envisioned himself alone with the Lady Jennifer, free to touch her where he desired. His body responded to the intriguing images playing across his mind. He tried to remember how furious he had been when she'd parked in front of his door, but it was no good.

"Are you coming?"

Startled, Christopher focused on Jennifer's voice, which suddenly seemed distant. He turned to find her moving briskly through the doorway that led into his library. "We need to move along pretty quickly," she called back at him. "We're scheduled to lunch at a pub just south of Edinburgh. And—" she cast a knowing look at him over her shoulder "—the notes

I'd prepared on Bremerley's interior don't seem to match up with your rooms.''

Now he did laugh. A booming laugh to let her know he had no regret he'd been found out so soon. Clever, clever woman indeed.

He hurried to catch up with her.

Listening to her lecture in earnest now, he was surprised by how much she knew of the history of the Borders, the Scottish county whose southern edge touched England, where the battles between the two countries spanned hundreds of years and had been the fiercest. Castle Donan had been a crucial link in the line of defense. She had exchanged hands a dozen times at great cost to both sides. He was so enthralled by her discussion he didn't at first notice one of the men moving apart from the group to investigate a pair of dueling pistols mounted on one wall.

Out of the corner of his eye, Christopher glimpsed a hand reaching up. A shout burst from his lips before he could stop it. ''Don't!''

Everyone turned to stare at him. Jennifer tipped her head to one side and observed him with a look of triumph sparkling in her eyes.

Taking three long steps across the room, Christopher moved the man's raised hand away from the pistol. ''The earl wouldn't like you touching his things,'' he said, trying to keep his voice level.

''Sorry, I wasn't going to hurt it,'' the tourist objected.

''That's an excellent rule to follow anytime you're in a museum or building of historic importance,'' Jennifer suggested cheerfully. ''Many items you'll see are irreplaceable, and age has made them fragile. Let's move along now.'' She flashed him a wicked

smile in passing. "I'm sure there are many more intriguing things to discover here."

By the time they had finished viewing the first
floor, Christopher was sure Jennifer not only knew
she wasn't in Bremerley, she also had determined he
wasn't who he pretended to be. He felt her watching
him whenever the little group entered a new room.
Repeatedly he caught himself standing between the
group and his most cherished possessions, as if un-
consciously shielding them from clumsy hands. He
was certain she added this mistake to her collection
of clues.

At last she turned to him as they circled back toward the great hall. "Are the rooms on the upper
floors open for viewing?"

He automatically stiffened at the thought of strangers plodding through his private chambers. "I,
well…you see, the upper floors are all under renovation." It was true, though he could have shown
them, anyway. All but the turret; that was his alone.

Two of the women standing nearby sighed with
disappointment.

"Well then, that's it for this stop," Jennifer announced. "Thank you, Christopher, for letting us in
and playing host. We've enjoyed seeing the castle."

"Anytime." His own voice, so relaxed and affable,
sounded strange to him. How long had it been since
he'd felt this free of tension?

Before he could count off the months, Jennifer was
herding her charges toward the towering doors, her
voice echoing against the stone as she efficiently announced their itinerary for the afternoon.

Christopher followed at her heels, feeling just a little guilty for having strung her along. It didn't matter

that he would never see her again, he thought as he stood and watched her group pile into the van. He just didn't like the idea of her going away, thinking he had intentionally tricked her when, really, his in-tention had been to help her out of a jam. And, of course, have a little innocent fun.

"Wait!" he shouted just as she started to slide into the driver's seat. Reaching in he pulled her out and closed the door to give them some privacy. He spoke in a low voice. "You figured it out. How?"

"Caretakers, usually, are only superficially loyal to their employers," she stated, her eyes turning unex-pectedly sharp and serious. "No hired hand takes as much pride in his boss's home as you obviously do. I was afraid you might throttle Mr. Pegorski when he touched that pistol." She looked him accusingly in the eyes. "This isn't Bremerley, none of the architec-tural details match my notes, and you aren't anyone's caretaker. So where am I and who are you?"

He gave her a stony stare appropriate for the lord of a trespassed manor. "This is Castle Donan. You took a wrong turn. I'm Christopher Smythe, earl of Winchester."

Her gaze didn't waver, and after a moment she nodded slowly. "I've heard of you, or seen your photo somewhere. A magazine, I think. One of those celebrity tabloids at a kiosk in London."

He lifted one eyebrow, unsurprised. "Don't believe everything you read." The fact that she seemed nei-ther impressed nor worried by his reputation intrigued him. He lifted her fingertips to his lips. Gently he brushed across her soft knuckles. She smelled like vanilla again. After a moment he reluctantly released her hand.

"The earl of Winchester," she repeated thought-fully.

"A relatively minor title. They hardly recognize me at court."

She looked doubtfully up at him from beneath a pale fringe of lashes. Jade behind silk. "Right. You're just an average Joe who fades into the woodwork...or stone, as the case may be."

He shook his head and smiled—a real and full smile, for the first time in as long as he could remember. For some reason it pleased him that she considered him attractive. He had learned to ignore looks from female admirers, except for those remote instances when his body told him it was time. Time to satisfy the urges a man could never quite escape.

"You're not a very good liar, you know," she said. "And you don't look at all like a servant. I suspect you couldn't fool anyone for long."

He liked her refreshing candor. "The inability to deceive can be a good trait. How long will you be in Scotland?" he asked, impulsively.

"One more day."

"And then?"

"We'll be in London two days, then I'll send my charges back to the States. I've planned to stay on for an additional day before leaving myself."

"So little time. A pity," he murmured as she turned to open the van's door. An unwelcome heat settled down low within his body.

He chose to ignore it. Clearly Jennifer Murphy was on this side of the Atlantic for only a brief time. Her home and future lay in the U.S. His place was in Great Britain and would remain so for many reasons he chose not to dwell on now.

"Well then," he began, but had to clear a strange roughness from his throat before continuing, "good-bye, Jennifer of Baltimore." He offered his hand, then helped her up into the driver's seat before turning quickly in the direction of his stables. He needed a good hard ride. It wasn't the physical activity of his choice, just now, but it would bloody well have to do.

Jennifer glanced up at the rearview mirror as she drove away from the wrong castle. For the few seconds it took the van to reach the first curve in the drive, she watched Christopher Smythe stride around the corner of the gray stone wall of his beloved Donan. Her palms felt moist on the steering wheel. Prickles teased the back of her neck. She could still feel the pressure of his lips against her fingertips. Damn the man.

Yes, he was arrogant. Yes, he was too good-looking and rich for his own good or the sanity of any woman who crossed his path. But thanks to him, no one in her party seemed to realize she'd gotten lost on her way from London to Edinburgh, and intruded on a real earl and his home. For that she was indebted to him.

How could it have happened? She *never* got lost! By the time she led a tour, she had done her home-work—charted her routes in detail and double checked them, memorized her lectures on the art, architecture and history for each stop.

She was vexed with herself, so much so that she didn't blame him for tricking her. Admittedly he had taken advantage of her mistake and flirted with her outrageously, but he had also provided a way for her to save face. She really ought to do something nice for him in return. Maybe send a thank-you note...or rip up at least one copy of that horrid tabloid that had written embarrassing things about him.

Throughout the afternoon in Edinburgh, Jennifer thought about Christopher, even though she tried her very best not to. His dizzying blue eyes flashed repeatedly in her mind; his expressive mouth and sexy British accent whispered to her as they toured the ruins of Hollyrood Abbey and the adjoining park. She remembered how his dark hair had fallen in a boyish wave across one corner of his forehead, and how his eyes twinkled, sharing the joke with her when he realized she had found him out.

Then there was that fingertip-kissing business. Had the seductive tingles racing up her arm been unintended? Probably. Christopher was a man accustomed to—and obviously very good at—arousing such feelings in women. But he no doubt had gone through the motions automatically. She could picture him bussing the plump hand of an octogenarian duchess, then turning unconcernedly away as she swooned. All in a day's work for a handsome earl, what?

Although Jennifer's head told her the feelings he'd left her to sort out meant nothing, her heart wouldn't cooperate. *Now is the worst time to complicate your life,* she told herself.

She had to protect her own and her mother's financial security. That was her first priority, and it meant working long hours to pay off the last of the debts her father had dumped on them before her mother finally divorced the rogue. It would be nice to have a man in her life, yes. But none she'd ever met could guarantee her the security she needed. And she'd be damned if she let one come between her and the financial well-being she needed!

Jennifer thought about her father, then about Christopher. The only type of male worse than a womanizer with a penchant for gambling was a playboy who threw money away on extravagant clothes, cars and parties for his friends. And he lived on another continent! Imagine the weeks of separation, wondering if he was spending his last pound or sleeping with another woman while they were apart. Even if he was faithful to her, imagine the money wasted on long-distance calls and airfare.

Getting hung up on someone as sexy and charming as the earl of Winchester—who lived in an honest-to-goodness castle, raced the length of polo fields astride wild-eyed ponies and made women weak-kneed at the touch of his lips…that would be the worst mistake of her life.

Stop it! Jennifer ordered herself as she shakily gripped the iron rail outside the bleak stone walls of Hollyrood. Why on earth was she thinking like this? She had spent exactly ninety minutes in the company of Christopher Smythe. She knew next to nothing about the man, and here she was daydreaming an already-doomed relationship with him! She must be losing her mind.

At the end of the day, Jennifer made sure that everyone in her charge was well fed and settled into their respective rooms at the stately Caledonia on Princes Street. Bringing her maps and brochures with her, she took the lift down to the hotel pub and found a seat in a quiet corner. There would be no more mistakes made on this trip! With a determined little cough, she unfolded the city street map of Edinburgh.

"Good idea," a deep voice stated from nearby.

Jennifer looked up, startled. "What are *you* doing here?" She grinned at Christopher, her insides quivering with pleasure at seeing him again, even as an inner voice whispered, *Don't you dare get all wobbly inside!*

"Business," he said quickly. "Need a second opinion on those maps?"

She laughed. "I suppose it wouldn't hurt, although we'll be walking most of the time tomorrow. I don't know what happened today. I *never* get lost, honest. If my mother ever found out she'd have a fit."

"Then we won't tell." He winked at her and pulled out the chair beside hers. Leaning over the table, he scrutinized another of her maps, the one showing Scotland's highways, one of which she'd highlighted in bright orange.

"Is Donan the real name of your castle?" she asked. She had noticed earlier that he pronounced it as a Scot would: Dun-in. "I couldn't find it on the Historic Registry."

"It's taken from the Gaelic, the name of an ancient clan. I haven't yet been able to qualify for the registry, because of its condition." He pointed with one long finger at a symbol on the map. "Here was today's problem. You should have waited for the next exit off the A7, just after the loch. Then you would have been fine."

"I know, I figured that out when we stopped for lunch. I really do feel foolish. By the way, I owe you for covering for me. Although most of the folks in

my little crew are very nice, I have one problem couple.'' The rest of the group was easy.

She had four couples, three of which were married
and seniors. The other couple was in their thirties and
evidently had been dating for several years. The remaining two clients were a single man in his forties,
who was tracing his genealogy, and a fiftyish woman
who seemed to enjoy the security of traveling with a
group.

He frowned. ''What kind of problem?''

''They're never satisfied with anything, or at least
they pretend to be upset. I have a feeling they're
building up to ask for their money back. We guarantee satisfaction with all our excursions.''

''Surely just one little slip like getting lost for an
hour shouldn't cost the entire holiday.''

Jennifer shrugged. ''You'd be surprised. Some people sign up for trips knowing they can get at least half
their fees refunded if they complain loudly enough.
It's a scam of course. But sometimes it doesn't pay
to let them drive away new business, especially if
you're a small company like us. You just have to take
the loss.''

Christopher shook his head.

She studied him. The irises of his eyes were a
darker, more intense blue here in the pub. She sensed
a serious side to him that hadn't been as evident at
Donan. He had a habit of locking his jaw when he
was displeased with something—like the unfairness
of con-artist travelers and thoughtless guests who
dared touch his treasures.

''You're not just in this hotel by coincidence, are
you?'' she asked intuitively.

He looked up from his glass of whisky. It was half-gone, and she suddenly suspected that, whether or not business had brought him to Edinburgh, he had been waiting here for *her*. The thought sent a warm, liquid shiver through her body.

"How did you find me?" she asked.

"It wasn't difficult. When you climbed in your van to leave, a brochure from the Caledonia lay on the passenger seat. I figured the odds were good you'd be staying here tonight. If I hadn't found you in here, I would have called up to your room."

A pleasantly nervous chill rippled up her spine. "And did you have any particular reason for tracking me down?"

He studied her, his lips firmly closed, his expression verging on severe, brooding. It took him a long time to answer. "I guess I just wasn't ready for the tour to end."

"You were the one who said the other rooms in the castle were off-limits."

Slowly his mouth relaxed into a wicked smile. "Not *that* tour."

She could feel the heat filling her cheeks like the diluted pink wash from a watercolorist's brush when touched to paper. The way Christopher was looking at her felt dangerous, in a delicious sort of way. She told herself that her reaction was because she was so far from home, on foreign territory...alone. And she wasn't accustomed to receiving propositions, if that was what this was, from castle-owning aristocrats. How many women were?

Jennifer looked down to find Christopher's hand pressed warmly over hers on the tabletop. Desperately she tried to force her brain to function, tried to come up with something witty and sophisticated enough to impress an earl. Her mind was a maddening blank. A second later, it kicked into gear, only to deliver a troubling question. Does he have a girlfriend? She had seen his photo with a long-legged, spa-polished woman in that London tabloid. Had his companion been more to him than a simple date?

"Does this sudden silence mean the tour has ended?" he asked at last.

She smiled brightly and aimed for a politic line. "If you ever visit Maryland, be sure to drop in on us in Baltimore. I'll show you the sights."

"Those aren't the sights I'm most interested in seeing." His eyes. *His eyes* were impossible to escape. They drew her in. She tried to pull her hand away, but his fingers closed tightly around hers. Her pulse throbbed in her throat.

"Let's try this again, luv." The last word, which sounded more Liverpuddlian-Beatles than upper-crust British, took her by surprise. Christopher leaned across the table and looked into her startled eyes. "No more beating around the bush. How about going out to dinner with me tonight?"

"I've already eaten." The words tumbled out of her mouth before she had a chance to consider whether or not she wanted to fib herself into a second meal.

"We could go somewhere for dessert and coffee," he suggested.

Jennifer stared down at their clasped hands. She was beginning to be able to read him, which was a little scary after knowing him for so short a time. What she understood from his voice and body language was that Christopher Smythe wasn't going to take no for an answer. And if he refused to listen to the word, where food was concerned, what did that tell her about his willingness to understand and honor her wishes when more was at stake than overeating? Her only countermeasure was to seek neutral ground, fast.

She looked around at the dark wood paneling, bronze sconces casting their golden light, the beautifully aged leather banquets, the other guests conversing in hushed tones—a classically masculine setting, very British, very earlish. Ver-r-r-y Christopher. But all that mattered to her was that it seemed safe here.

"I have an early morning tomorrow," she said. "Why don't we just stay here and talk."

He appeared neither pleased nor disappointed. "Fine. What will you have to drink?"

"A white zinfandel, please."

His hand barely raised above the level of the table before the steward appeared beside him. Moments later a glass of pale pink wine was set before her. Jennifer took a few cautious sips, and mellow warmth enfolded her.

Christopher settled back in his chair and observed her over the amber liquid in his own glass. "Why Baltimore? Why do you live there when you've obviously seen so many exciting cities?"

"I live in Baltimore because it's my home," she said simply, then came back at him. "Why do you live in Scotland when you're English?"

He seemed startled by her question, and the muscles in his jaw visibly tightened. "I live in Scotland because I like it," he responded brusquely.

Not satisfied, she set her wineglass on the table between them. "That's no answer. Everyone chooses to do things because, for one reason or another, they find them appealing.''

"Not always. Sometimes we act in a certain way because we have no choice."

"Everyone has choices."

"Not always," he snapped. Then, as if he thought he might have spoken too harshly, Christopher reached out for her hand again and rubbed his thumb soothingly over the back of it, creating a warm spot. "Life sometimes surprises you," he said enigmatically.

Jennifer decided the level of tension in the air dictated a change of subject. She asked the first question that came to mind. "What are your favorite London restaurants?"

He seemed to welcome the new direction of their conversation. As he spoke, his voice grew less tense. She watched his thumb trace hot little circles over the back of her hand, entranced by the motion as much as by his touch.

At one point she caught a glimpse of him in the mirror beside them, and she thought to herself— though it didn't seem logical at the time—*this is a tormented man.* But how could that be when a man had so much money, so many friends, so many opportunities in life? She dismissed the thought as overly romantic, far too Jane Austen: the lord, the castle, the dark moods.

When she turned back to face him, he was studying her and had stopped speaking.

"What?" she asked.

He shrugged. "You're so pretty and so American."

She didn't know how to react to the compliment, or was it a subtle dig? She sipped her wine and de-

cided to address the second part of his statement.
"What's that mean—to be *so* American?"

"You have an optimistic, nothing-ventured-
nothing-gained attitude." His eyes still seemed shadowed with sadness, regret or resentment...but they
warmed as he looked at her. "You'd be fun to be
around, Jennifer. You would make me laugh, and I
would tease you until you blushed, everywhere." His
glance dropped suggestively to the front of her
blouse.

She was so shocked, she didn't know how to answer. But his gaze created a lovely pool of heat in
her center. She liked it. Liked all of the sensations,
even though some of them might be risky. Nevertheless, when Christopher brought his eyes up along her
throat to her face, she met and held them with her
own.

"I'm sorry," she whispered. "I'd really like to get
to know you, too. But I'm working for as long as I'm
in England, and I'll have to leave soon."

"Yes," he said. It was the only time she remembered hearing a single word sound wistful. He lifted
his glass to her. "Here's to missed chances, luv."

Two

Jennifer decided to take her breakfast alone the next morning. Room service was a small luxury she felt justified allowing herself. She needed time, a telephone and no interruptions to complete her plans for the remaining days of the trip. Just as the tray with her breakfast arrived, the telephone rang. She tipped the waiter and dashed across the room to answer.

"Good morning! I was hoping I'd catch you before you left for the day."

"Christopher?" Her heart raced at the rich timbre of his voice. Her fingers threaded through the coils of the telephone cord, twisting them tighter. She'd lain awake all night wondering if she'd done the right thing by brushing him off.

"Did you sleep well last night?"

"Absolutely," she lied energetically. "Was the drive back to Donan very bad in the rain?" It had started to pour at ten o'clock, just after he had left her.

"I ended up staying in the city at a friend's place."

She couldn't help wondering about the gender of that friend, but immediately told herself it was none of her business. A man like the earl undoubtedly had social connections in most every city in Europe. Some were bound to be with attractive and wealthy women—a good match for him.

"My business is going to keep me in Edinburgh longer than I'd expected," he continued. "But I won't be able to accomplish much of anything until the afternoon. I wondered if you'd mind my tagging along this morning. I'd make myself useful, help out with the driving if you like, give a running narration as we move around the city."

"That would be nice," she admitted as calmly as possible, while her heart hammered out a wild tattoo in her chest.

"That isn't to say you didn't do a beautiful job at Donan." His voice slid lower, became subtly inti-mate. "You are a remarkably insightful woman, for one so young."

She looked down at her fingers, which were hope-lessly snarled in the cord, and decided she must be imagining the change in tone. "You can only get so much out of books," she said quietly. "A person has to live in a country to really understand it. You have that advantage over me."

For a moment neither of them spoke. Then he seemed to rouse himself at the other end of the line.

"What time shall we meet?" he asked.

"Nine o'clock in front of the hotel. If you like, you can arrange for the valet to bring the van around."

"That I'll do, lass," he said, in a fine imitation of a Scottish brogue that set her grinning.

Jennifer hung up the phone. Her hand was trembling, and the nape of her neck felt damp with perspiration. Why did he affect her so strongly?

She had met plenty of interesting men, but she wasn't prone to being swept away by the mere touch of a hand or flash of blue eyes. Was she afraid of that dark inner core of him? No, she answered herself. Christopher seemed to be a man with principles. If he'd been truly dangerous, the gossip columns would have had even more ruthless comments on his flamboyant lifestyle.

So, yes, he was flirtatious, but she was certain he would never attempt to force her to do anything against her will. Was he the sort of man who got his kicks seducing female tourists? She'd run into that type before—identified, cataloged and dismissed them without hesitation.

No, she decided, Christopher Smythe was different. But what made him different and what he wanted from her—those were the real questions.

Despite her preoccupation with the earl, by nine o'clock Jennifer had finished drafting her plans for the day, selected the appropriate maps and guide notes she'd written up before leaving Maryland and called each of her clients' rooms to make sure they were ready to set out. True to his word, Christopher was waiting beside the rental van when she stepped outside, followed by most of her group.

"Oh, it's that handsome young groundskeeper from the castle!" one of the women twittered.

"*Dashing,* dear. Here in Britain, all the young men are dashing," another woman corrected her. "You

know he looks an awful lot like that young lord we
saw in that newspaper in the hotel lobby.''

"I wonder what he's doing trailing after us to Edinburgh," Mr. Pegorski commented, waggling his
eyebrows in Jennifer's direction.

She pretended not to see or hear any of them.
"Everyone, this is Christopher Smythe from the castle yesterday. You remember him, of course. He's
agreed to give us a local's view of the city."

Jennifer could feel the estrogen level rise in her
group as the females ogled Christopher. The rest of
their party arrived then, so they all piled happily into
the van and started out for an overview of the city.

While Christopher drove, she sat beside him in the
passenger seat and studied his profile—elegant, but
purely masculine, she decided. His features were
powerfully drawn; his blue eyes made the more vivid
by the dark lashes outlining them. A very faint scar
ran close to the hairline along one temple, and she
wondered if it had been caused by a polo injury. The
article she'd seen mentioned his aggressiveness on the
polo field. From the little she knew of the game, it
was a rough sport requiring strength and daring. His
hair was a dark, glistening brown that verged on black
when out of direct sunlight.

She admired his speaking style, which combined a
touch of dry humor with crisp intelligence, all
wrapped up in an English accent she found irresistible. But over all of this was a veneer of a darker
emotion—like mahogany laid over paler oak—disappointment or sadness, or something fragile she
couldn't yet define.

"Do you have family around here?" she asked between stops along their route.

He seemed startled by her question, then glanced sideways at her, still keeping an eye to the road as they sped along. "My father still lives in Sussex. I have two brothers." His voice was clipped, to the point.

I'll wager they're both as devilishly handsome as you, she thought. Were they as terse and secretive, too?

"Then your brothers live in Sussex as well?" she asked.

"In Sussex? With my *father?*" He choked on an involuntary laugh. The taut muscles in his face relaxed enough to allow a thin smile. "My father isn't the kind of man who encourages his family to remain close to home. As soon as we were old enough to be away from our nanny, he shipped us off to boarding school. None of us have gone back for more than the occasional holiday."

"How old were you then...when you first went away to school?"

"Six."

"Six years old!" She knew that the upper-class English put great stock in educating their youth away from home, but a six-year-old seemed hardly more than a baby to her. "Didn't your mother object?"

The corners of Christopher's lips pinched grimly inward, and she knew she'd said something terribly wrong. But before she could apologize, he was speaking in that incredibly dry, unemotional way she was beginning to suspect might be his form of self-protection. "Apparently, her sons' welfare wasn't at the top of her list of priorities. She left my father and the three of us before I turned a year old."

"I'm so sorry," she whispered, shocked at the very

idea of a woman abandoning three sons and a husband.

"It's all right. I remember nothing of her." The
chill in his words was a thing she could almost touch.
His pain showed in the fine lines around his eyes and
mouth, despite his unemotional denial. She didn't
know what to say to comfort him, but she sensed she
had to keep him talking or risk losing the one chance
she might have of understanding him. For some reason, that seemed important to her.

"Are you and your brothers close?" she asked
hastily.

It took a moment for him to gather his thoughts
and answer this time. "Not in any way you might
expect. My oldest brother, Thomas, is an advisor to
the King of Elbia. He lives with the royal family,
travels with them, rarely returns to England. He re-
cently married an American woman and inherited a
gaggle of youngsters in the bargain." He chuckled
affectionately. "Thomas has his hands full now, but
seems happy as a clam in an ocean of mud. Our middle brother is Matthew. I think he took our mother's
desertion the hardest. He was three years old when
she left, and swears he remembers her vividly. As
soon as he turned twenty-one and collected his inheritance, he lit out for America. He's been there ever
since, running an import business."

She waited for Christopher to go on. Something in
the halting way he had spoken told her that he wasn't
accustomed to talking about his family. When he
didn't continue on his own, she prodded gently. "Do
you often travel to visit your brothers?"

"I have obligations here," he said, casting her a
sharp, sidelong glance.

That was it then. He was ending the conversation.

"I see," she murmured. But she didn't, not really. What was more important than family?

Elbia, she mused, as her clients chatted happily among themselves in the seats behind her. She tried to envision a simple map of Europe. Wasn't that the tiny alpine country about the size of Monaco? How difficult could it be for a man with Christopher's means to jet across the continent for a quick visit with his brother? Traveling to the States was a little more difficult but surely the business that kept him tied down in Scotland would allow for a few weeks off now and again to see his own family.

"What are your plans for the rest of the day?" Christopher asked after a long silence.

"Edinburgh Castle, of course, then Queen Mary's Bathhouse and the Royal Mile for shopping and house tours."

He glanced up at the sky. "The rain should hold off long enough."

She nodded, then let a grin slip out.

"What is it?" he asked, glancing at her curiously as he pulled over a lane to let a lorry pass.

"Queen Mary of Scots. Legend has it, she bathed in white wine and goat's milk. I wonder if that mixture really is good for the complexion." She held her arm out to inspect it as the truck sped past them.

"I'll bring the wine and milk, you try it out and—" he lifted a dark brow aimed toward the dip in her neckline "—I shall be the judge."

She laughed, thinking she wouldn't put it past him. *Stand ready for inspection, miss!* He'd insist on seeing every inch of her. Fat chance she'd let him!

Christopher accompanied Jennifer's group to the

castle and sixteenth-century cottage known as the queen's bathhouse, which, more likely, had been a simple summerhouse or dovecote. He then asked her to drop him off at his car and arranged to meet them after lunch.

Jennifer watched him drive off in a bottle-green Jaguar, weaving expertly through the noonday traffic. She promised herself that when he returned she would find out one more thing about him. Just *one* more thing before she let herself like him any more than she already did.

So far, she had been careful. She had done nothing wrong. It was all just talk and a little flirting, the way strangers do—particularly when one is from out of town. Talk, harmless glances, a few touches. That was all.

But she felt in her bones that he wanted more. And, in truth, so did she. She wanted him to run his thumb in those little circles on the back of her hand. She wanted him to call her ''luv,'' in that playful, un-aristocratic, bad-boy way. She wanted him to touch her where his eyes had suggestively rested as they discussed Queen Mary's baths.

All this, even though she knew in her heart that they had no more than a few days to share. But first she had to know if there was another woman in his life.

As Christopher drove out of the city in the Jag, his thoughts turned from one female to another. Lisa was the most precious thing in his life. Yet she had never really belonged to him. Ever since he had learned he was to be a father, eight years ago, he had set aside

all else for the child. Whatever was best for her came
first.

When a woman he had had a brief affair with told
him that she was going to have his baby, Christopher
initially had been shocked and troubled. He immediately offered to marry her, only to discover she wasn't
interested in marrying him. His masculine pride took
a hard hit, but another part of him was relieved. He
knew he didn't love her, and she was quite honest
about her lack of feelings for him.

"Our marrying," he remembered her saying
coldly, "would be stupid. I've already told Sir Isaac,
my fiancé, about the problem. He's fine with it. Really. As long as we publicly let on that the baby is
his, for the time being."

At first this had seemed fine to Christopher. He'd
been let off the hook. But when Lisa was born, he
couldn't stay away from the hospital. And at the instant his gaze settled over her tiny pink face and crys-
tal-blue eyes, he lost his heart. From that day on he
had done all he could, without going back on his
promise, to see his little daughter and support her in
any way he could.

He became an official friend of the family. As soon
as she could speak, Lisa took to calling him Uncle
Chris. If he was lucky, the nurse would bring the little
girl down to greet houseguests, which often numbered
in the dozens. Lisa grew from fragile infant to delightfully rambunctious toddler, to a charmingly in-
telligent child who favored wearing her riding jodh-
purs and helmet over white eyelet and pink ribbons.
He never tired of talking to her or reading her stories.
And she always seemed just as happy to see him.

When she was old enough to go to school, he offered to pay her tuition. All her mother had to do was choose the school. Much to his dismay, instead of selecting one of the better London institutions, Sandra Ellington chose her own alma mater in southern Scotland. So very far from London, where he lived.

Determined not to lose contact with Lisa, he had secured a position for himself on the board of regents at St. James School for Girls. He had been present at nearly all school functions in the past year that she had attended, particularly when Lisa's mother couldn't be, and he dropped in on the campus whenever possible. He aggressively solicited funds for the new addition to the school from his many social contacts while sharing Lisa's triumphs with pride.

Time passed so very quickly. Christopher prayed for the day when Sandra would do as she had promised him years before and tell her daughter about her real father. "I'm just waiting until she's old enough to comprehend all of this. It's a delicate issue for a young girl," she reminded him whenever he asked.

Now he was beginning to wonder if she ever would reveal his identity to Lisa. Fear alternated with helpless anger. His hands were tied, his silence expected, and emptiness gnawed at his soul.

He knew it wouldn't be right to act without permission from the child's mother. After all, she must understand her daughter better than anyone. What if he risked revealing all to Lisa, and the girl refused to believe him? Their warm relationship would be destroyed. Worse yet, she might feel betrayed because he had lied to her all of these years, pretending to be an honorary uncle when he really was her father. She might hate him. He couldn't bear that.

And so he continued to wait and hope for a time

when he could embrace his daughter and tell her how much he loved her...had always loved her.

As it turned out, Lisa's class was on a field trip that day and he couldn't see her at all. Disappointed, he picked up his copy of the builder's contracts for the addition from the administration office, then drove back into the city. He would need to review them before the board meetings. The urge was stronger than ever to cherish and protect the little girl who might never know his secret burden.

"The Royal Mile was wonderful!" Jennifer cried when she saw Christopher waiting for her outside the Caledonia. "I bought a ton of great stuff, and I almost never shop while leading a tour!"

He had been under such an oppressive cloud since he left St. James that he'd feared his spirits would not be lifted even by seeing her again. But just the sight of her sunny face and sparkling eyes did wonders for him. She gave him something other than his troubles to think about.

"I'm glad," he said, at the moment more interested in the lovely glow of her cheeks than her shopping victories. An intriguing thought shot unbidden through his mind. Just how far down her body did that glow extend? The length of her long, sweet throat was rosy with excitement, but her collar stood obstinately in the way. Would her breasts be flushed as well?

He felt himself react to the image, then immediately warned himself to get a grip. He liked her; she excited him. That, after all, must be the end of it. When he was younger, he had effortlessly picked up girls and, if they were willing, made careless love.

American coeds had been attracted to his English accent like moths to the proverbial flame. And when he let slip his title in casual conversation…instant meltdown. A quick hop into bed.

But after Lisa came into the world, he took sex far more seriously. His liaisons became infrequent, cautiously and safely executed. He had learned he wasn't the sort of man who could spread his progeny with abandon. He considered himself responsible for little Lisa.

There was also a change in the way he allowed himself to feel about women. If they were so easily able to enjoy one man's pleasures then go off with another for reasons of prestige or money or pure flightiness, he would never again let himself feel anything enduring for one of them. It was a matter of self-preservation.

But Jennifer was incredibly desirable. She would tempt any man to throw off caution as quickly as a topcoat at the first bloom of spring. He must be careful…very careful, he reminded himself.

Having completed the afternoon's tours, the group had returned to the hotel for a hearty meal. Early-evening excursions had been arranged by those wanting to pack more into their day, while others discussed going to the theater or a quiet game of cards in the lounge.

"Looks like you'll have some time to fill before turning in," Christopher said after Jennifer bade her crew a good evening.

"Yes," she said. "But I need to check in with my mother and pack for London."

"I see." So tomorrow she would indeed be gone. He sighed inwardly. In the little time he'd spent with her, she'd been good for him. When he was with her, his thoughts seemed lighter, the day somehow brighter, more tolerable. He dwelled less on his mistakes. Or maybe that was all romantic hogwash, and he just wanted to sleep with her. A good dose of lust definitely took a man's mind off his troubles.

"Thank you for all you've done," she murmured, laying her hand on his arm, making him even more aware of the sweet scent wafting up from her skin. She stood close to him. So close he could easily slip his arm around her waist and pull her against him. Right here in the lobby. Why not? "Everyone has said," she continued breezily, "what a wonderful treat it has been, your taking us around today."

He forced out the correct, civil words and even gave her a polite smile. "No trouble at all. I enjoyed myself."

She beamed up at him in appreciation, and he thought he had never liked green eyes as much as he did now. "Yesterday...I was serious about my invitation. If you ever do come to America, and you're near Baltimore—"

"It's unlikely," he said, interrupting. "You can do me another favor, though." He hadn't thought through his words. They simply arrived on his lips, and he had no power to stop them.

"Anything," she said. "What is it?"

"You wouldn't have dinner with me last night. What about tonight?"

She blinked thoughtfully. "I'm not sure I should."

"Why not? You're free for the night. You need to eat, don't you? I know all the best places in Edinburgh."

"But—"

"You're leaving tomorrow. I'm not asking for a lifetime commitment." Lust was a charmer, he was. The muscles in his shoulders and back tensed as he waited for her answer. *Don't say no...don't say no!* a voice chanted from inside of him. "I'm harmless," he added, flashing her a deliberately wolfish grin.

She laughed out loud. "I'm not sure of that part." Still, she hesitated. "Listen, I don't know any tactful way of asking this, but... Are you attached in any way?"

He chuckled. "You mean married? Good Lord, no."

"I meant...*seeing* anyone."

"No. Although I do keep the phone numbers of a few ladies who graciously accompany me on social occasions. Would you like references from them?"

Jennifer rolled her eyes. "I'm sorry, it's just, you never said and—" she shrugged, looking prettily flustered. "Yes, I'll have dinner with you. You pick a good place to eat."

"I know the perfect one," he said.

Two hours later Jennifer was certain she'd made a mistake when Christopher pulled his car off the A7 and onto an unpaved road that looked suspiciously like the one leading to Donan. "I thought we were going to your favorite restaurant."

"My favorite place to eat isn't a restaurant."

"You can cook?" she asked.

"No," he admitted. "I have a wonderful woman who prepares my meals. When I was given a choice of the family's estates as part of my inheritance, I chose Donan. Half the castle was in ruins, as it still is, the other half hadn't been occupied in years and was in need of serious renovation. But I wanted it, and the Clarks, who had been with my father for years in Sussex, have kin in the area and were eager to take it on for me."

"You're lucky you can run your business from a place like this."

"Yes," he said quickly.

Having already seen the first floor, she knew the way to the dining room and turned in that direction as they passed through the great hall.

Christopher touched her on the arm. "Hold on a moment. Let me check with Mrs. Clark to see how close our dinner is to being ready."

Jennifer wandered into a side room and contentedly browsed along the dark-paneled walls. When she had been here with her group, Christopher had pointed out one of Alexander Nasmyth's oils of a Borders landscape. The mist-enshrouded body of water in the center looked a lot like nearby Loch Kerr. Then there were two portraits that appeared somewhat older, in the opulent style of John Wright, though she was no expert on seventeenth-century art. For all she knew they might actually be Wrights—in which case they'd each be worth a small fortune.

She followed a narrowing corridor and found a canvas whose artist she was sure of—one of her favorite painters, Anne MacBeth. Anne had been a member of the so-called Glasgow Girls, at the turn of the previous century, who had rocked the art world with their daring experiments combining art nouveau and Celtic influences. Jennifer was delighted. Either Christopher or someone in his family was a serious collector of female artists as well as the established masters.

Christopher returned, smiling when he found her in

front of another MacBeth painting. "We can sit down now. It's ready." He stood behind her and rested his wide hands on her shoulders when she lingered just a moment longer in front of the painting. Jennifer felt comfortable beneath his steady palms. "I was going to take you around the rest of the castle, if you'd like, but since the meal is hot and you're hungry..."

"I am famished," she admitted. "But I'm curious about the upper floors. I would love a tour after dinner." She wondered what other treasures might be hiding in dim corners or forgotten rooms, waiting to be brought out into the light.

They ate wild duck, prepared with a deep red Burgundy sauce she would have thought a more likely match for beef. It was a surprisingly delicious combination. They drank a local wildflower wine from Cairn O'Mohr, which seemed perfect with the meal. She had never eaten game before. At home, everything in her fridge came from the supermarket, and most of that was in the form of frozen commercial dinners. She favored quick-and-easy, low-fat meals. Tonight the textures and colors on her plate resembled an artist's palette, and the flavors were amazing. She savored every bite.

"I must tell Mrs. Clark how wonderful a cook she is."

"I'm afraid she's left for the day," he said. "I told her I'd wash up after we finished eating. It didn't seem fair to make her stay while we indulged ourselves in a leisurely meal."

Jennifer smiled. "That was nice of you." She caught a mysterious twinkle in his eyes and wondered if his motives for dismissing the woman were all that pure. Sending the staff home to leave their master alone in the castle with a female guest...this had all the makings of a classic seduction. She wasn't sure whether she was more nervous or excited at the prospect.

For dessert there were buttery cookies filled with high-country jam that Christopher insisted on calling biscuits despite her arguments. And there was steaming dark coffee, laced with heavy cream and a touch of hazelnut liqueur. Jennifer felt contentedly full at the end of the meal. They sat and talked for a while longer, then she helped him remove the dishes to the kitchen and rinse them before placing them in an enormous stainless steel dishwasher.

"For parties," he commented when he noticed her staring at the mammoth machine. "It holds service for up to fifty."

"Very modern for a castle," she commented. "Do you entertain a lot?"

"Friends come up from London quite often, to hunt and generally laze around."

She wondered how many of those hunting/lazing friends were of the female variety and single, then reminded herself she had no reason to feel even the tiniest bit possessive. Soon Christopher would be out of her life, and she would be out of his. They were from two different worlds, and she was returning to her own after a day in London.

He led her back into the foyer, then took her hand and started up the stairs. "Time for your tour," he said, sounding eager at the prospect.

A wave of heat swept through Jennifer at the image they made, climbing hand in hand up the elegant marble staircase to the private chambers above. They were alone in the house. Music from the dining room rose along the staircase, as if carrying them upward on the delicate notes.

By the time Jennifer reached the top, she was out of breath.

"Sorry, did I take it too fast for you?" he asked.

"No, not at all." She swallowed and gulped down two breaths…then two more. "I walk every day for exercise. It was nothing."

Chris frowned at her, his dark brows lowering in concern. "You aren't afraid of me, are you?"

"You? Heck no," she lied brightly, then rattled on. "I'm just excited, I guess. I love old houses, and this beats anything in Baltimore by a good four hundred years!" But she was nervous, being alone with him here in this ancient, remote place when she still knew so little of him.

He smiled. "Good. Let's start on the right side of the corridor, work our way down the hall, then come back up the other side." He seemed to hesitate. "If you have energy left, we can climb the turret."

Jennifer's eyes widened. "A real turret?"

"Very," he agreed. "Come along. You can tell me what you think I should do with these rooms. Most still need a great deal of work."

Jennifer was astounded by the rugged beauty of the ancient structure. Although modern plumbing and lighting fixtures had been added over the years, and softening touches—miles of plush carpeting, billowy draperies and immense hanging tapestries—increased the comfort of the building, tons of stone still dominated. It exerted an intensely masculine influence over every room. She felt the power of centuries of English kings and Scottish lords who had battled over Donan, won her, then lost her to the next man. She imagined the haunting presence of their ladies, too. Women who were protected and loved by their husbands and masters, or perhaps suffered cruelly at their hands.

History changes little, she mused as they strolled from room to room. Men fought for what they believed or longed to possess; women loved and sometimes suffered for their choices in a man. Christopher's ancestors, Englishmen, had come to Scotland and laid siege to this place...then held on to it, no doubt against fierce opposition. She sensed in him that same sort of determination: to hold on to the things he cherished, to be strong in the face of adversity, to fight for what was his.

Christopher opened yet another door, and she stepped through to find a tightly wound spiral of steps leading up into endless darkness. "What is this?" she asked.

He flicked on an electric fixture, sending a blaze of yellow light up a shaft constructed of granite blocks. "This is the north turret, the only one still standing after the last siege in the eighteenth century. When I was a boy, we sometimes spent summers here. Now I've made it my private apartment."

She looked up to see a veil of serenity already descending over his features. This was a special place for him, she sensed. A healing place? But what did a man like the earl of Winchester, so strong and in control of his life, have to heal from? His mother's desertion? It must be something more recent than that.

Another, different sort of thought flashed across her mind. How many Scottish lasses had been invited or ordered to climb these stairs by Christopher's ancestors? Was she following in tragic footsteps? Her nervousness returned.

Christopher's hand moved up against her back, coaxing her forward. But she couldn't make herself move above the bottom step.

"Do heights frighten you?" he asked.

"No." *But being alone with you, up there, might,* she added silently. "Maybe we should go back down now. It's getting late," she murmured.

He turned her toward him and frowned down at her. "Is something wrong, Jennifer?" When she didn't immediately answer, his eyes narrowed with suspicion. "If I'd wanted to attack you, don't you think I would have done it before now?"

"Oh no, I wasn't thinking—"

"Yes, you were." His eyes were intense, piercing, the darkest blue she had ever seen. Something close to a night sky. She shivered under their gaze. "You've read too many gothic novels, luv. Here—"

Before she could pull away, he looped one arm around her waist and pulled her tightly against his body. His lips settled tenderly over hers then deepened briefly into a warm kiss that set her head reeling.

It was over as quickly as it had begun. She fell back against the stone wall, gasping for breath, gazing up at him and wondering why his face was suddenly out of focus. Her knees threatened to go.

"What was that for?" she gasped.

"To prove I could kiss you without being driven mad by passion."

"I see." As to her own passion or sanity, she couldn't presently vouch for either. But she did know that her heart was thudding like crazy in her chest, and lower down she felt a pleasantly urgent tingle. *Oh, my,* she thought. *What a pity I won't be around for more kisses like that!*

"Jennifer. Are you all right?"

She stared up at him, feeling suddenly impish. And in the mood for taking risks. Big risks. "I'm fine. But I think it only fair that I should prove the same to you."

He looked intrigued. "I don't find you particularly threatening, but if you like..."

She stepped forward, lifted her arms and reached up around his neck. Quickly she tugged him down to her level and centered her mouth over his. Then she did something she hadn't planned. She parted her lips on a blissful sigh as they kissed.

Christopher took advantage of the invitation and ran his tongue across her teeth. He tasted marvelous. An intoxicating mixture of heather, smoke and wine. He tasted like a man she wanted to touch and be touched by. It had been a long time since she had been with anyone; her last boyfriend had been only the second of her entire life. They had broken up over two years ago when he had been transferred across country by his employer.

She had missed the touch of a man's hands. But she also missed the practical aspects of a relationship, like having someone with whom to share a meal, see a movie or kiss on New Year's Eve. However, she hadn't deceived herself into thinking she had ever been in love.

But now...now Christopher Smythe, a man she'd known less than two whole days, was kissing her in delicious ways she'd never been kissed before, doing things to her heart that felt as perilous as they were delightful. And there was no promise, not even a fool's chance of extended companionship to follow a night of intimacy.

As if Christopher had just had the same thought, he suddenly pulled away.

No, she pleaded silently, *not yet. Don't stop yet!* His arms...his mouth, they had felt so amazing.

"Come on," he whispered against her ear, the touch of his breath sending little shivers down her spine as he clasped her hand in his. "You'll like the view from the top."

She liked the view just fine right here! Midnight-blue eyes, muscled jaw set against a backdrop of weathered gray stone. Just fine.

Still in a daze, she let him pull her up the graceful swirl of granite. She could no longer feel her legs, and barely noticed when each step came up beneath her foot. Her heart beat faster the higher they climbed. Her palms grew moist, slipping along the iron rail bolted into the curving wall.

Jennifer stopped being afraid halfway to the top. Why was she fighting herself? She *wanted* him to touch her; *needed* to learn what the hand that held hers would feel like caressing her body. Nothing else seemed to matter.

The final step opened into a circular floor covered with thick crimson carpeting. The walls had been paneled in mahogany, and leather-bound books were arranged neatly on shelves that curved halfway around the single room. She turned, taking in the entire space. It was furnished as a suite, with a bed in a sleeping area, desk near the bookshelves and a lamp table and love seat opposite. An open door revealed a small, private bathroom that, from a glimpse of shining modern fixtures, must have been added in the last few years.

Tall window casements looked out across the night.

She moved to the nearest one and gazed into the darkness, feeling profoundly alive—aware of every detail around her, every sound, every scent. Every beat of her own heart.

The sky was black and sparkling with more stars than she ever had seen in a Baltimore sky. In the distance she glimpsed headlights creeping along an invisible road. Farther away the electric glow of Edinburgh pinked the night sky.

"We're far enough from city lights to get the full effect of the stars," Christopher murmured.

"Yes. I can see that. It's lovely." She felt him step up behind her.

His strong arms wrapped around her and gently eased her back against his chest. She didn't flinch. Lightly his lips pressed down on the top of her head. "Do you like my sanctuary?"

"Very much." *I'd like it even more,* she thought wistfully, *if you'd kiss me again.*

For what seemed a long time, they stood just like that, staring out at a world that seemed to have melted in the darkness, leaving them with only each other. She sensed that Christopher was thinking deep thoughts, making decisions for them—which was good, she decided, since she was incapable of thinking rationally.

At last his voice broke the magical silence. "I'll drive you back to the hotel as soon as you like. I just wanted to share this with you."

She turned in his arms and gazed up at him, puzzled and more than a little disappointed. "That's the only reason we came up here—the view?"

He gazed warily down at her. "If the situation were different…" He let the thought go.

"Different in what way?" she asked.

"This isn't something I can discuss with—" He sighed, shook his head in frustration.

"With a stranger?"

A sudden chill descended between them, and he stiffened. "With a woman who will be gone before the end of the week," he said tightly.

"I see." Jennifer didn't know how to respond or what he wanted from her...or even what she expected of herself. Stepping out of his arms, she moved away to clear her thoughts.

Jennifer scolded herself for having behaved foolishly. She knew better than to get involved with locals while traveling. At home in Baltimore, she never would have let herself get carried away like this on a first date. She was falling headfirst into an old trap—the vacation fling. An unwise temptation for any woman.

Her glance drifted past Christopher's shoulder to a photo on a bedside shelf. A young girl wearing a school uniform smiled into the camera. Jennifer tensed. Was that what he had meant by, "if the situation were different?" Did he have a child? Despite all she thought she knew of him, might he secretly be married or living with the child's mother.

All the lovely warmth drained from her body. "You'd better take me back to the hotel now," she said.

"Certainly." But he didn't move. And she didn't dare look at him. "Jennifer?"

"Yes?" When she reluctantly brought her eyes up to meet his, she knew he'd followed her troubled gaze to the framed portrait.

"I told you—there is no one else. I'm free and clear."

She felt numb, then hot all over. "Oh."

"I know that you need to leave, but I really want to kiss you just one more time."

She swallowed. "You were right the first time. We shouldn't."

"I know." He reached out and, grasping her wrist, hauled her into his arms. "To hell with being right."

She had no will to struggle. Everything drifted away except the sensations of his body pressing against hers, his lips moistly caressing hers. Her only reality was the shocking physical energy passing between them. She spread her fingers across his crisp, white shirtfront, stretched up on her toes and let her head fall back as he opened his mouth over hers.

Jennifer curled her hands into fists against his chest as she felt his hand move up and close over her breast. The warmth of his palm penetrated her blouse and bra; she ached to feel his fingers touch her flesh instead of fabric. He must have had a similar thought. A second later he was tugging her blouse loose and slipping his hand beneath it. As his palm molded the cup of her bra, he paused and looked into her eyes, as though asking her permission.

She nodded.

His strong fingers moved beneath the nylon lace. His palm warmed her breast then moved aside just enough to gently roll her nipple between thumb and forefinger. She gave a little yip of pleasure, arched against him and felt his arousal against her stomach.

"You're like silk," he groaned, dropping his cheek against her forehead. His breath was hot and labored.

"I want you, Jennifer. I'm sorry. I didn't plan…make me stop if you don't—"

She pressed her fingertips over his lips, silencing them. "I want you, too," she whispered. But his few seconds of doubt had sharpened her own thoughts. She wasn't as experienced as many women, but she understood that heartbreak was sure to follow an affair as sudden and hot as theirs promised to be. "But this isn't going to happen, Chris. We must stop." The words came out strong and reasonable, despite her body's protests. *You don't sleep around,* she told herself. *If there is a man to love in your future, he won't be a one-night stand in a foreign country.* "Can we just sit and…hold each other?" she asked. Maybe his arms around her would be enough.

He didn't answer at first. She waited, not moving within his intimate embrace. At last he seemed to have composed himself. "If you like." Slowly he withdrew his hand from inside her blouse.

She closed her eyes and tried to prolong the warmth of his touch. If only her body would stop quivering and her head remain clear for longer than a few seconds. Darn hormones, she thought ruefully.

"Come here," Chris said, holding out his hand to her. He led her to the Victorian love seat. Sitting with his back against one pillowed arm, one leg extended along the cushions, he brought her down so that she could lean back against his chest. With his arms enclosing her, she felt as near to heaven as she'd ever been.

"Rest," he whispered, touching his lips to the pale wisps of hair on top of her head. "It will be all right."

"We'll go back to the hotel soon," she murmured.

"Yes, soon." He stroked her cheek, and his breaths grew quieter, deeper.

Jennifer closed her eyes and let the earl soothe her. She still ached for him. But this would have to do.

Three

___

Christopher's first conscious thought was that his back hurt like hell. He tried to recall if he had taken a bad fall during his last polo match, but didn't think he had. His second thought, still before he'd opened his eyes, was that something rather heavy was sitting on his chest. Not as heavy as a horse, thank goodness, so he was probably okay. Then a faint whiff of vanilla met his nostrils…and he knew.

Jennifer. Not sitting on him, sprawling over him.

His eyes flickered open. Through the window he could see a gray predawn sky smudged with the first streaks of rose. He was stretched out on the love seat in his turret apartment. Jennifer was curled peacefully against his chest, her eyes still closed.

Smiling to himself, he stretched his aching spine against the cushions of the short couch and buried his nose in the soft blond tresses feathering his cheek.

Apparently the earl of Winchester had spent the night with a beautiful woman, he thought whimsically. His smile widened. Regrettably, the usual advantages attached to such a statement had not come to fruition.

Jennifer stirred in his arms. He automatically contracted them protectively around her body to keep her from tumbling off the couch. After a moment she turned her head to squint up at him. "Tell me we didn't."

"I think I'd remember if we had. And I sure hope you would." Christopher let his eyes drift closed again, enjoying the feeling of holding her. He knew it was selfish, but he wanted to keep her there with him, despite her plans to leave for London that day.

She touched a fingertip to his morning-whiskered cheek. "Christopher."

"Hmm?"

"I'm sorry. You need to wake up and drive me back to the hotel…now."

"Now?" He sighed, bear hugging her until she let out a little grunt of protest. His mind was racing, seeking ways to convince her to stay, even if for just another hour or two. They could make love as the sun showed its new face. He would touch her in all the ways, on all the secret places he'd imagined touching her last night.

"Christopher?" Now she was sounding just a bit irritated.

Short of brute force, he decided, there was no way of holding her there. "I suppose we might as well face the music," he grumbled. "I wonder what your traveling companions will think when they discover their valiant leader has slept with a man on their first date?" He grinned mischievously at her.

Jennifer smacked him on the thigh. "We have *not* slept together—not that way, at least! Now let me go. We have to get back to the hotel before I'm missed. Breakfast isn't served until seven, and most of them won't come down until eight. It can't be any later than six now. I think we can make it."

She started to push herself off him. But he liked teasing her too much, and he locked his arms around her all the tighter. "And I thought you American women were easy."

"This…this isn't funny," she sputtered, struggling…but not, he noticed, too energetically. "What if one of my clients needed me during the night?"

"They aren't children, luv."

Jennifer jumped at the sexy little word. It wasn't the first time he'd used it. Before, she'd thought it a charming affectation; it made him more human, less like an aristocrat complete with title, castle and a heap of very old money. But that was before they'd kissed and…well, before he'd touched her bare breast. The intimate memory sent a shiver down the back of her neck, clear to her bottom. No, she was being ridiculous. It was just a harmless appellation used by the English much like her Baltimore neighbors used "hon" even when addressing a perfect stranger. No real sentiment attached.

"I have two seniors with heart conditions," she reasoned. "And one who is prone to occasionally forgetting what planet she resides on. They're easy enough to manage when I'm with them. But I'm *not*. So don't tell me not to worry."

He released her with a theatrical groan. She leaped up and ran to the cheval glass mirror to finger comb her hair. With a quick wipe of a fingertip beneath

each eye, she banished the shadowy traces of yesterday's mascara.

"Fine, fine. I'll take you back." He caught her eye
in the mirror and winked wickedly. "But if we get
caught, it will be a shame we didn't enjoy the pleasures of our ruined reputations."

Jennifer tossed him a poisonous glare.

"Can't blame the lord of the manor for trying,
m'lady."

"I suppose not. Young aristocrats are expected to
lead loose, perverted lives."

"We are?" He stood up and patted his pockets,
frowning.

"Of course. Everyone reads about the rich and ti-
tled all the time in those scandal sheets. Prince of
Macadamia Caught in Tryst with Chorus Girl! Royal
Couple Takes Separate Vacations...but Not Alone!"
She followed him around the room as he hunted down
what she suspected would be his car keys. "Royals
out-Hollywood movie stars. My mother dotes on their
escapades."

He laughed as he bent to scoop the errant keys off
the floor from beneath the couch. "Is that so?"

"I'm not as fascinated with your type, myself."
She sniffed delicately for effect, elevating the tip of
her nose. "I think people should behave decently no
matter who their parents are or how many figures describe their bank accounts."

"Come along, Miss Prim and Proper," he said,
grabbing her hand and marching into the stairwell. "If
you want to return to your flock before daybreak,
we'd better get a move on. There's a more proper
WC on the floor below, if you want to freshen up."

She hurried after him, all the way down what she

was sure must be a hundred steps to the ground floor. After a quick stop at the bathroom, she met him outside.

The early-morning mists off the lake had sparkled the grass and flowers with dew. It still wasn't quite light, and the air held a milky quality, a thickness that made her want to reach out and gather soft handfuls of it. She breathed deeply of its sweetness, so different from the air surrounding her dear old Baltimore, as often rich with exhaust fumes as the scent of blooming honeysuckle. Here, the atmosphere begged to be inhaled, savored, held in memory.

"I'm not a rich brat," Christopher said after they had driven a mile or so.

She slid farther down in the supple leather of the Jag's passenger seat and yawned lazily. "Did I say you were?"

"You implied as much back at Donan. What was your description of my life? Loose and perverted?"

"Well, you *do* live in a castle," she stated accusingly.

"That's not a crime or indication of decadence. Donan is my legacy from my ancestors. I could let it crumble, sell it or sink a lot of money and back-breaking labor into restoring it, which is what I have been doing over the past few years."

"Really?"

"Really. You should have seen its condition before I moved up from London. When the place is fully renovated and furnished, I hope to open it as a museum and memorial to both the Scots and English men and women who gave their lives fighting for it. It's never too late to mend fences, don't you agree?"

She considered this new side of him. "Your friends

are all in London, at least that's where their permanent homes are?''

"Most of them, yes."

"Why don't you just hire workmen to handle the restoration while you run along to whack polo balls with your chums? You obviously can afford it." She had wanted to tease him, but he seemed not to take the remark with the good humor it had been intended.

His eyes turned stormy. Long fingers tightened on the steering wheel. "I have my reasons!"

She observed his expression. Something told her she should stop right now, but she couldn't. "Is one reason your daughter? The little girl in the picture."

Christopher didn't answer for several minutes, but finally resigned himself to admitting what she had already guessed. "Yes, that's Lisa. And she is my daughter." He steered the Jag onto A7, north toward Edinburgh. "Now, if you please, we won't talk anymore of her."

The terrible thought occurred to Jennifer that the child might have died, and she'd innocently reminded him of the pain of losing her. Or perhaps something else had come between them. For a moment she was horrified by her thoughtless questions. But then she replayed his words in her mind: "That's Lisa." Present tense. And the photo looked quite recent. So at least it wasn't death that caused him such anguish.

She ached to ask him a thousand questions, but his icy glare had locked on the highway, and she knew that no amount of prodding would elicit another word from him on the subject of the child in the photograph. His face held that closed expression. Just as it had the day she'd mistakenly driven up to Donan, thinking it was Bremerley. *No trespassing.*

They arrived at the hotel just after the sun had fully risen above the horizon, chasing away lingering pastel wisps of morning's first light. Neither had spoken for the remainder of the drive. Sadly Jennifer reached for the Jaguar's door, but before she could slip off the leather seat to the ground, his hand closed around her wrist.

"Wait, Jenny." There was a provocative urgency in the way he had shaped her name into a more intimate version. Warning tingles raced through her body. She turned apprehensively on the seat to face him.

"What, Christopher?"

"I don't want this to be goodbye." He looked as surprised at his own words as she felt at hearing them.

Now she forced each word to sound calm and logical, even though her heart was thudding wildly in her breast. "I don't think we have a choice about this goodbye business, Lord Smythe."

He was shaking his head before she finished. "I have to meet with several people in London. It could wait until next week, but since you're heading that way—"

"I don't know," she said warily.

"I can be an asset if you'll let me." A wicked grin spread across his lips.

"Or a distraction," she added dryly.

"There's nothing like a native guide when traveling in a foreign country." He dipped his head and peeked up into her face, almost managing to look boyishly innocent. "Your clients liked my Edinburgh travelogue."

She laughed. "Is this the line you use on all female

tourists? Come along, dearie, I'll show you the sights."

"I'm serious, Jenny." He took her hands in his. "Let me see you again. Just until you leave England. It will be fun, I promise. And I won't get in the way of your doing your job."

She sighed. It seemed useless to argue. Time and miles would ultimately separate them. What difference could another day make? "Oh, all right. I assume you have a place to stay."

"I'll book a room at your hotel."

"Your *own* room...not mine," she stated clearly. He winked at her. "'Course, luv."

Although it was a good seven-hour drive from Edinburgh to London, time seemed to speed by, thanks to Christopher's dramatic tales of old-time reivers, as the Border raiders were called. He pointed out Roman ruins, ancient woolen mills, historic houses, abbeys and battle sites as they passed.

At their hotel in the West End of London, Christopher offered to help unload luggage while she checked her party in. But when the desk clerk handed her the keys to pass out among her group, she stopped and counted them a second time. "There are only keys for six rooms here."

"Yes, madam," the clerk agreed. "Just as you requested."

"We requested seven. I have four couples, two singles and myself. Seven."

The man looked worried, and her stomach responded with a sharp pinch. "What's wrong?"

"I'm afraid we are fully booked for the night."

Jennifer gasped. "What?"

Christopher came up behind her. "Having problems?" She turned to see he had settled her people in the far corner of the lobby with their mountain of suitcases and hanging bags.

"It seems we're short one room. And they have no space for you."

"There are other hotels nearby," he said.

"It's unlikely any will have vacancies, sir," the clerk said apologetically. "The city is full for the exhibition."

"Ah," Christopher said, nodding. He turned to Jennifer. "I'd forgotten. The International Art Exposition. Everything will have been reserved for months ahead."

"What can we do?" she whispered, stepping away from the desk to let others register. She stared hopelessly at the keys in her hand, then at the elegant art deco lobby with its marble mosaic floor and gilt cornices. It would be rude to ask any of her people to double up on rooms. The tour had been advertised as a luxury adventure. A cozy, private ensemble—but not *that* cozy.

"I have a thought," Christopher said. "Just listen before you say no, because it may be the only way."

She nodded.

"Give your room to one of your party. That will allow each of them a private room as promised."

"What about me...and you?"

"I have friends who own flats all over the city. I expect at least one will be out of town. We switch off houses frequently. Give me a few hours, and I'll have a key."

She pursed her lips in a schoolmarmish pout, and he thought she'd never looked more appealing. But her eyes...her pale-spring-green eyes looked worried. If she hadn't told him she'd had boyfriends before, he'd have described them as virginal.

"Relax." He patted her hand. "I'll be the perfect gentleman."

She watched him disappear through the etched-glass doors of the chic London hotel, unsure why she felt she had been rescued from one crisis, only to be tossed into the jaws of a far graver situation. The ship was sinking...thank God for the life boat—but now the sharks are circling.

It had been just chance, right? Christopher certainly couldn't have planned...no, of course not. It was simply a coincidence that the hotel had gotten the reservations wrong at a time when the city was mobbed with visitors. In a way it was great luck that Christopher had been with them.

But she didn't need the temptation of sharing a private apartment with the man. No, she didn't need *that* at all. Whenever he came near, her body seemed to shift into a higher gear. All he had to do was fix her with those amazing eyes—Parrish blue, she thought. Named for the artist who had become so famous for that intoxicatingly rich hue. She felt a subtle anticipation take over.

As for Christopher, she didn't know what he was thinking about their arrangement. He liked to flirt, and obviously enjoyed the company of women. But he hadn't pressed his advantage at Donan. She decided that whatever urges she felt probably weren't shared by him. Somehow, she'd have to work out her own tangled emotions, if not in London, then after she returned home.

For now, Jennifer concentrated on the job at hand.

She explained the situation as diplomatically as possible to her party. No one seemed particularly concerned about her alternate accommodations except Mr. and Mrs. Kiley, the complainers, who didn't disappoint. She saw everyone to their rooms, made sure they each had a copy of the itinerary for the rest of the day and arranged for a meeting time after a few personal hours for shopping or a nap.

While she waited for Christopher to return, she sat in the hotel lounge and ordered tea and biscuits for herself, less to satisfy her appetite than to encourage a clearer state of mind. Before she knew it, she would be on a jet heading back to the States, and Christopher would remain in England. The problem was, she reminded herself as she sipped her steaming Earl Grey, not only were they from opposite sides of the Atlantic, they were from two vastly different cultures and economic backgrounds.

He was passionately involved in restoring one of his family's historic homes. But he was doing it without regard to cost or his own living expenses. The business he'd spoken of wasn't anything like Murphy's Worldwide Escapes. It was personal business. He had no real "job." If she chose to stop working and do whatever amused or interested her, she'd starve within a month. Christopher, on the other hand, entertained lavishly, owned a small herd of polo ponies and collected priceless artwork.

She didn't begrudge the man his pleasures, but his fast, unconventional lifestyle troubled her, and the possibility of becoming involved with a man like that terrified her. Her father, by spending frivolously and shirking honest work, had destroyed their family. His gambling debts alone had nearly ruined her mother's business and nearly lost them their home. His womanizing had shattered her mother's heart. A thousand times over Jennifer had sworn she would never let herself fall under the power of a man like that.

Yet last night she had come alarmingly close to sleeping with just that sort of person. A man who combined her rascal father's worst traits, only on a higher fiscal level! They both had a weakness for horse flesh; they both had their magical ways with women. Sighing, she sipped her tea. It was definitely a good thing she hadn't given herself to the earl of Winchester last night. Definitely.

Christopher picked up the key to Geoffrey Montgomery's flat from his neighbor. He let himself in, opened windows to air out the place and checked the fridge. Supplies were low. He decided to pick up a bottle of wine, some fresh fruit, a wedge of cheese—perhaps a good Stilton or Cheshire—and a half dozen fine, spicy English bangers. Just enough to tide the two of them over should they need a late-night snack. Half an hour later he was back with the groceries, feeling cheerfully domestic as he stocked the refrigerator.

Christopher returned to the hotel to find Jennifer gathering up her crew to tour the National Portrait Gallery. He excused himself to deal with his own business but met up with them before they left the hotel for dinner. Because she'd reserved tables at The Wembley a month before the trip, there was no trouble getting everyone fed. The atmosphere during the meal and after was exuberant, and her clients all seemed well satisfied with their day's activities.

Christopher had left the Jag back in Edinburgh, so

he drove Jennifer in the van to his friend's flat and parked on the street.

She gazed up at the elegant slate-gray building. "It looks almost like a Baltimore rowhouse, only not brick," she commented.

Christopher watched her out of the corner of his eye as they ascended the steps to the front door and let themselves in. The flat was on the second floor by British reckoning, two levels above the street, and there was no lift. It was an older building, but prized for its location in one of the trendiest parts of the city. He had promised himself, as well as her, that he wouldn't misbehave. But in the last few hours, misbehaving with Jennifer was all that had crossed his mind.

During dinner, Christopher had several times caught himself staring into his own cupped hand, imagining the way her breast had filled it. He managed to stop himself from openly staring at those lovely attributes that men with manners weren't supposed to acknowledge in public. But, in unguarded moments his eyes rebelliously drifted toward her tight little bottom and the swell beneath her blouse.

Now, as they entered the flat, his pulse drummed in his ears. His mouth grew dry and fingertips twitched. He stepped into the middle of the room after locking the door behind them, acutely aware of her breathing, the whispery sound of her footsteps across the carpet, the crisp way she moved into this foreign territory. She was taking stock of the place, as he was taking stock of her. He wondered how long he'd be able to keep his hands off her.

"Are the bedrooms this way?" she asked, peering toward a closed door.

"It's through there, yes." Damn it, he didn't care what he'd promised her. He had never wanted a woman more than last night and now. So what if she wouldn't be around for long after! If his pattern of interest in women proved consistent, he'd sleep with her once, maybe twice, then the heat would be gone and with it his interest in her.

He became aware that she was glaring at him, her hands propped on her hips in a sure sign of displeasure. "Yes?" he asked.

"*It? One* bedroom?"

"This was the only option available," he explained with a shrug.

She looked doubtful.

"I swear." Her implication didn't seem fair. He might be secretly lusting after her like a pillaging heathen, but he hadn't intended to force her to sleep in the same bed with him. Although, at the moment the idea seemed an entirely acceptable one. "Everyone who wasn't in town has let out their places to friends for the exhibition."

"And you plan to sleep where?"

He had to laugh at her skeptically arched brow. She could do that proper-young-lady look so well. He would love to walk straight up to her, tear off her conservative white blouse and stand back to enjoy her reaction. He had a notion that behind all that determination to behave herself, she was burning to be touched. He would be delighted to oblige.

"This isn't the least bit humorous," she said.

"Of course it is. Do you suspect every man you meet of conspiring to get you into bed?"

She blinked at him, and he wondered if she was

disappointed or just surprised that he'd come out and said it. "You mean you're not?"

"I won't claim innocence. It isn't that I wouldn't welcome the opportunity to join you between the sheets. It's more a matter of having already given up the battle."

"Oh." She nibbled pensively at her lower lip, then looked away. Her shoulders gave an almost imperceptible quiver. If this was a woman who didn't want to be loved, then he must have lost all ability to read female body language.

"You, woman, are driving me mad," he muttered, suddenly overcome by a vital need to kiss her.

In two swift steps he closed the distance between them. Embracing her before she had a chance to dance away, Christopher brought her to his chest. His lips closed demandingly over hers. He expected her to push him away. If she had, he would have let her go immediately and apologized, even though he wouldn't have meant it. But she didn't push, and he had no willpower left to make the effort himself. Then her mouth opened beneath his, and that sign of welcome was far too exciting to pass up.

He loved how sweet she tasted. He delighted in the sensation of her body melting against his. When they had kissed before, he told himself that was all that could ever happen between them. A simple kiss. No more. Then he had caressed her breast, and he'd drawn another mental line beyond which he swore he wouldn't step. Now his mind stopped functioning entirely, stopped laying down rules and limits, stopped demanding he do anything but follow his instincts and satisfy his hunger for her.

He would feel himself inside of her. *He would.*

Her voice came to him, as if in a dream, through the blinding heat of his passion. He made himself pay attention despite his body's insistence that he not listen. "Please…" she whispered urgently.

Please…*what?* Was the next word, *stop?* Or *more?* It was a lousy time for the woman to forget how to speak in complete sentences!

With other women there always had been a spiritual distance, a separation between emotion and the physical act. Everything seemed obvious then. The message he got from their bodies, their eyes, their hands was easy to interpret. They had come to his bed to indulge their own desires. Consequently, the sex they shared had satisfied his needs. Staying together for any length of time had not been an issue.

Jennifer had appeared out of the mists of Loch Kerr in a funny red van. She had charmed him before he realized what was happening. He had been too busy flirting and playing tour guide to realize that he was feeling something real and special for her. And now, as he held her, he understood it was too late to step away without causing himself, and maybe her, as well, considerable pain. But it had to be done. It was the honorable thing to do.

He started to push her away, but she clung to him.

"I don't want to hurt you," he whispered in her ear. "I didn't plan this. Believe me."

"I don't care," she whimpered, but he wasn't sure what it was she didn't care about. About her leaving him? About having sex with a near stranger? About his motives for bringing her here?

Still frantically turning over possibilities in his mind, he felt her clasp his hand and bring it timidly to her breast, as if asking him to take up where he had left off the night before. He groaned and squeezed his eyes shut, searching for the strength to tell her no. No, he wouldn't make love to her.

But his willpower was depleted.

Holding her trusting gaze, he unbuttoned her blouse and slid his hand inside, beneath the lacy cup of her bra. Her nipple was warm and flat, but hardened immediately against his palm. Low in his own body, he felt a familiar tightening sensation.

Christopher looked down at her breast, naked and white against his sun-bronzed hand. "How beautiful," he murmured, and bent to touch his lips to the quivering rosy circle beneath his thumb.

She arched against him and shuddered. He licked the tight nubbin, then drew it between his teeth and savored her flesh. As if the bones in her lovely limbs had dissolved, she started to slide from his grasp. He supported her, not wanting to move, not wanting to stop doing what he was doing as he took her other breast and warmed it in his mouth. If ever there was a woman he wanted to bed, this was the one. He'd have plucked her from among thousands.

Through the heavy, steamy haze of his desire, Christopher told himself he should move slowly, not expect too much from her too quickly. He must give her a moment to look into her heart and stop him if she had second thoughts. Although, he prayed she would not. She hadn't touched him at all yet, and he longed to feel her hands over him.

Taking her fingers, he gently pressed them suggestively between their hips. She turned her palm toward him, shaping it over him through his trousers. Even through the textile barrier, the effect of her touch shocked his system. He groaned at the insistent throb.

"If you mean to change your mind," he whispered hoarsely, "please be kind enough to do it very soon."

Jennifer stared up at him, her eyes wide. They were the most sincere and innocent he'd ever seen in a grown woman. "I can't tell you why...but I want this," she whispered.

He closed his eyes briefly in thanks. He didn't know what he would have done if she had told him to leave her, now that she'd driven him so high.

His hand trembling, he moved it toward his belt buckle but she stopped him. "Let me?"

He smiled. She was perfect: curious, frightened, eager, shy and daring...all wrapped up in one delicious woman. If his emotions were in a whirl at this moment, hers must be in a maelstrom. Selfishly he decided he liked his storm, and he would let her weather her own.

She slid down his zipper and slipped her cool fingers inside but hesitated at the edge of his briefs. "It's all right," he said softly, "if you don't want to." He would survive, he supposed.

His words seemed to give her courage. Her hand moved beneath the stretchy waistband, and she found him.

"Oh, my," she breathed as she wrapped her slender fingers around him.

He grew in her grip, but steeled himself against taking his own pleasure, for the time being. First he must see to hers. He felt her hand moving tentatively along him, as if she was testing to make sure she was doing it right.

If you only knew, luv, he thought, gritting his teeth with the effort. He didn't know how much longer he could hold on.

He ran his hand up her thigh, beneath her skirt. She was wearing his least favorite feminine garment— panty hose. Ignoring the nylon web, he molded his hand over her and pressed gently, learning the shape of her, planning his path. She whimpered again, softly, rested her head heavily against his chest and returned the pressure against his palm.

"Please…"

"What do you want, Jenny?"

"My knees feel… I can't stand up any longer."

He swept her off her feet and strode with her in his arms to the bedroom. It seemed an endless journey, although it was only twenty-five feet and seconds away. Depositing her tenderly on the bed he stood over her impatiently as she pulled off layers of clothing, her eyes wide and just a little bit fearful even as they sparked with excitement. So many emotions within her, so many within him. But the last thing he wanted to do now was discuss feelings.

"Come," she whispered, moving over on the bed to make room for him. Her eyes were a vivid emerald, beckoning.

She was so lovely. She didn't have a model's figure. Hers was far better from his perspective. An alluring pair of pert breasts with tiny nipples, a waist that was trim but not starved, hips that rounded to coax a man's palms to them. He wanted to flip her over and study her reverse side, knowing he'd find it as enchanting and erotic and irresistible as this view of her.

She reached toward him, her eyes pleading as if she feared his hesitation was a sign he might bolt. Then he was stripping off his own clothes, tossing them wherever, heeding only the inner voice that drove him to her alone, for reasons he couldn't understand. He barely had the presence of mind to retrieve his wallet and a crucial item from it before joining her on the bed.

Christopher lowered himself over her, supporting the weight of his torso on his elbows, letting the fullness of his manhood rest against her. Just rest there for the moment…as he enjoyed the anticipation, caressed her smooth shoulders, absorbed the light in her eyes, understood her female cravings—which were demanding but delicate and still wary. She couldn't know after so short a time that he would never do anything to hurt or embarrass her.

She trusted him. How amazing.

All the more so because, he sensed, it hadn't been like this for her with other men. Jennifer was that rare woman who guarded her intimacies, cautiously dispensing them. All the more reason to live up to her trust. He took a moment to open the sealed foil envelope that he'd carried nearly forgotten in his wallet for months.

"Tell me if I do anything you don't want me to do," he said solemnly after he had taken care of protecting her.

She nodded, her eyes enormous, glistening, fixed steadily on his.

Easing her silky legs apart with his knee, he shifted his body to find her. Gently, he moved himself around the tender lips protecting her feminine center, until he felt her moisten and blossom. Her eyes closed in concentration and her fingers curled into his shoulders as she pressed herself upward to meet him.

Christopher slid within her, telling himself he must hold on, hold on, *hold on*…until the smooth undulations of his hips coaxed her to climax. She bit down on her lower lip, shuddered with each slow thrust and, at last, let out a gasp of surprise and delight, her eyes wide. He watched with satisfaction as pleasure washed over her sweet features.

After that he remembered few details. His touches, her responses, all wove a blazing tapestry of passion. He might have shouted out her name before giving himself permission to share her ecstasy, or perhaps that urgent plea had only come from his own fevered mind. He felt her beneath him, buried himself hard and deep within her, and gave himself up to the flames.

Four

Jennifer woke, her body still tingling delightfully from Christopher's lovemaking. In all her life she had allowed only two men to touch her intimately. Her first experience had been the summer after she had graduated from high school, with a boy she had known since fourth grade. They had lost their virginity together.

Her second lover had been her only serious boyfriend. They had dated in college and after, for a total of three years. Then he had been transferred by his company to Chicago. Eventually the long-distance telephone calls and cuddly e-mails had stopped, and she'd known that it was over. In a way she had been relieved. Eddie was a dreamer, not the sort of young man she could trust her future to.

Jennifer lay on her side, still naked, her bottom tucked into the warm male space between Christopher's muscled stomach and his equally hard thighs. He was relaxed now, breathing deeply, hovering in a shallow sleep. She smiled and wiggled herself in deeper, loving the feeling of his chest pressed to her back, his arm draped up and around her shoulders. Tucking her into him. Keeping her there. Never had she felt so safe and cherished.

They lay there for another half hour, until she could wait no longer to get up. Showers had to be taken. They would have to drive back to the hotel. A final morning of sight-seeing remained before she could take her group to Heathrow and bid them farewell. Then she had one more day to herself in London, making arrangements for her next tour.

Christopher stretched and squinted up at her as she extricated herself from his limbs and the warm sheets. "Come back here," he growled.

She laughed at him. "If I do, I have a feeling you won't let me out of that bed for another hour or more."

"Bloody well right," he grumbled. "Come here, woman. I want to—"

"I know what you want, and it will have to wait," she retorted lightheartedly. "There's breakfast at the hotel. Then I'll be tied up with my clients until I deliver them to the airport around noon."

"I have to wait *that* long?" he groaned.

"Yup."

"Bullocks."

Jennifer grinned and strolled into the bathroom. This was delightful. They had made love most of the night, and Christopher still wanted more of her. She showered quickly, humming happily as the steaming water splashed over her, then opened the bathroom door to let out the steam.

"I wish I could extend my trip, but my flight leaves tomorrow afternoon," she called out to him.

"Double bullocks."

"But there's no reason you can't come to visit me," she said, swishing peppermint mouthwash. "I was serious about your coming to Baltimore. You could stay at my place. It would be great fun!"

She listened for his answer, expecting an enthusiastic *Yes!* But not a sound came from the other room. Jennifer frowned into the mirror.

"Chris, have you fallen asleep again?"

"No."

She didn't like the tightness of his tone. Turning away from her reflection, she wrapped the towel more tightly around her torso and walked back into the bedroom. "What's wrong?"

Christopher had pulled the sheet to his waist and was sitting up in bed, frowning at her. "I believe we're on two different wavelengths."

An ominous chill rippled through her. "Oh? Tell me your wavelength, I'll tell you mine."

"I already know yours," he said in a controlled voice. "Last night…wasn't just *last night* to you. It was supposed to be the beginning of something, right?" His eyes were an intense, demanding azure.

"Maybe," she said cautiously. "I wouldn't have slept with you if I didn't think you were very special…if I didn't like you an awful lot."

"I *like* you too, Jennifer," he said guardedly. His unemotional tone said it all. How could she have been so naive? She had to turn away from him so he wouldn't see the look of disappointment on her face.

"What you're saying is," she whispered hoarsely, "for you this was a one-night stand."

"Not precisely." Still that careful formation of words, as if he feared she'd become hysterical if he slipped up. "I had hoped to make love to you again, later today and tonight."

"But after that?" She risked a quick glance his way.

He winced. "What am I supposed to say, Jennifer? You know the reality of our lives as well as I do. You live and work with your mother in America. My home is here."

She desperately wanted to run from the flat— clothed or not. Run from the overwhelming shame of having given herself to a man who took her so casually.

"I have a daughter," he continued. "I have obligations to her, to her school and to my properties on this side of the ocean. I'm no more free to pluck up my roots and move to another continent than you are. So what's the use of pretending we might have a future?"

"I see," she breathed. It took all of her strength to get out those two little words.

But he was only half-right. It wasn't geography that ultimately kept them apart. It was her own deeply embedded fears.

She reminded herself of all the nefarious ways her father had ruined his wife's and daughter's lives. He had squandered their livelihood on horses, women and expensive clothing. And here was aristocratic Christopher Smythe, ten times more fascinating and seductive than her father ever had been.

"Of course you're right," she murmured. "I just thought...never mind."

"I'm sorry," he said. "I thought you understood. What happened between us was purely physical. Great chemistry, but no more than a—"

"A fling. A brief affair," she supplied for him and looked up to meet his eyes. "Right?"

"Yes." His gaze was steady, strong and determined. He obviously hadn't fallen for her as she had for him.

Holding back tears with enormous effort, Jennifer scooped her clothing from the chair and ducked back into the bathroom. Somehow she would have to make it through the next two days. Once she was back in Baltimore, she would find the strength to forget the earl of Winchester. It would take time and a truckload of distractions...but she would do it.

Christopher felt like hell as he lay in the bed, listening to the dull roar of Jennifer's hair dryer. No. Worse than that. It seemed to him that he'd been allowed a glimpse of heaven before it was snatched from him. He had reacted in the only way he could—he'd pretended he didn't care. And he'd hurt her feelings.

Foolish woman. A single night of intimacy, and she was bubbling on about transatlantic visits! What on earth was she thinking?

Yet the urge to stay with her was almost overwhelming that morning as he watched her leave, suitcase in hand. He simply didn't know how to handle such foreign emotions or how to salvage her injured feelings. He would have liked for them to part as friends.

Christopher spent the entire morning trying to puzzle out a way to patch things up between them, but came up empty-handed. He ended up back at her hotel, and waited there for her, hoping she'd return after delivering her charges to Heathrow. It was almost 1:00 p.m. when he spotted her.

"I think we should talk," he said, intercepting her halfway across the elegant lobby.

She didn't seem surprised to see him but slanted him a wary look. "A room has become available. I'm going to take my things upstairs. I'll be down in a few minutes."

Impatiently he waited for her, pacing the rich crimson carpeting, skirting potted palms and statuary. At last she stepped off the elevator, her posture perfect, her walk deliberate and confident, even though her pretty eyes were tinged with pink.

"Are you all right?" he asked, gently guiding her to a small divan flanked by two enormous ferns.

"Of course," she said briskly. "I just have a lot to do before I leave tomorrow. My next trip is only a month away. A West End theater tour. I have reservations to make for the plays, restaurants to book…" She was stringing words together so fast he had trouble understanding her. Her eyes were too bright. Her face too taut. "After that, there's the South American trip…unbelievably exciting…drifting down the Amazon. And the Alaskan cruise! We're looking into an Asian adventure, too, and—"

"Stop it, Jenny."

She gazed innocently up at him. "Stop what?"

"You're babbling. You know that I don't care where you're taking your next batch of customers. I suspect that isn't uppermost in your mind, either."

She lowered her eyes for a moment, then brought them quickly back to his. "My business is important to me," she murmured.

"I wouldn't suggest otherwise. I just think you're avoiding the issue at hand."

"Which is?"

"Us."

"I thought you said this morning that there was no *us*." Her green eyes snapped with challenge.

"There isn't. But I don't think you believe it."

"Oh?" She looked adorably smug. "Now you can read my mind?"

He sighed. Nothing he could say here and at this moment would make her see how impossible it would be. What she needed was a demonstration.

"Come with me this afternoon," he said impulsively. "There is a polo match, with a cocktail party afterward. I think you'll enjoy yourself."

He was lying, of course. She'd have a terrible time. Even he found this particular clique of moneyed snobs detestable. But he had reasons for remaining within their social circle, and now they might prove useful to him in another way. If he and Jennifer couldn't part as friends, there was one other way he could make her feel better.

"Are you playing in the match?" she asked hesitantly.

"Yes. And in the shape I'm in today, I'll probably end up bleeding all over the field."

Her eyes flashed. "Good, then I *will* enjoy myself."

Jennifer's breezy declaration that she would delight in his injuries might have made him laugh at another time. But he sensed that she actually meant it. In a way that was good. Hate was a far easier emotion on the soul than love. After a disastrous love affair, it could even be healing.

But knowing that she was cheering for the other team and hoping for his demise worked miracles on Christopher's aggressiveness on the field. He rode the Number 3, field captain's position on his four-man team that day, and he had never played better. Time and again he tore after the ball, his horse's sharp hooves digging up chunks of turf, his mallet swinging wildly as he leaned precariously out from his saddle. He scored five goals that afternoon, against some of his toughest opponents.

After the match he handed over Prince's Pride to the stable lad who had driven three of his horses from Donan earlier that day. Christopher strode across the field to where Jennifer was standing alone. He was muddy, muscle sore and exhausted—but triumphant and basically uninjured.

He had cleaned up today, making nearly ten thousand pounds. But every one of the checks would be made out to St. James or one of his other charities. And every penny of the cash would find its way into the school's building fund—along with his matching contribution.

"You didn't give the other side much of a chance," she complained. "Seven to two."

"We were handicapped by three goals, so we had to win by a good margin." He smiled wearily at her. Despite her determination to dislike him, and his determination to help in the effort, there was a flash of admiration in her eyes before she turned away.

"We'll drive to the house for the party. It's about

a mile away. The players will wash up there. I have a change of clothes in the car.''

She nodded. ''Tell me about your daughter.''

The question was unexpected and put him instantly on guard. ''What do you want to know?'' he asked stiffly.

''Where is she? Does she live with her mother?''

He had never spoken about this part of his life with anyone. But it seemed harmless enough in this case. Tomorrow Jennifer would fly out of his life, glad to be rid of him.

''Lisa attends St. James School for Girls, near Donan. She will spend most of the year there. For holidays and the summer, she will be at home with her mother.''

Jennifer frowned at the horse trailers and cars driving off the field ahead of them as Christopher spread a towel over the upholstery of his car seat to protect it from his muddy clothing. ''Then you never get to see her?''

''I see her when I am at the school. I'm on the board of regents and stop by often. I'm also a frequent guest at her mother's house when Lisa is there. She's a great little girl.''

Climbing into the passenger seat, Jennifer studied his shadowed expression, puzzled by what he was telling her. It didn't make sense. The man clearly loved his daughter, yet she never lived with him? Halfway to the estate where the party was to be held, the truth dawned on her.

She turned in the Jaguar's seat to face Christopher. ''She doesn't know. Oh God, Chris, she doesn't know you're her father!''

He glared straight ahead through the windshield,

his jaw clamped shut, his foot pressing down too heavily on the accelerator.

"Why haven't you told her?"

"It's out of my hands," he snapped. "Now if you please, let's change the subject. This doesn't concern you."

It shouldn't, she thought. Whether or not Christopher had any claim on his daughter's time or love shouldn't have an impact on her in the least. But it did. She felt his pain, like needle-sharp jabs to her heart, as he sat silently driving much too fast.

"I don't understand," she whispered. "Have you done something to lose your right to be her father?"

He looked angry, then less so…but still undecided. "I thought the arrangement best for her at the time. She was so little, and her mother wanted her to have a normal family. She had married another man before Lisa was born. He knows about the affair, about Lisa being mine. But Sir Isaac's a gentleman. He didn't make a fuss. Sandra promised to tell Lisa about me as soon as she was old enough to understand."

"And she is how old now?"

"Seven."

"But surely—"

"Enough!" he said tightly. "Now you know. I live in Scotland to be near my daughter. When her mother thinks it's the right time, I will have her at least a portion of each year."

Jennifer shook her head but said nothing more.

Christopher's hopes seemed so fragile. She could tell by his voice that even he was beginning to doubt the day he had waited for so patiently would ever come. If his child's mother hadn't kept her promise by now, something must have convinced her to keep the secret to the few people directly involved.

Jennifer didn't speak of Christopher's daughter again that day. But she soaked up the flavor of his life as she observed him with his friends. The women were sophisticated, bright. Even those who weren't naturally beautiful managed to appear striking and desirable. The men carried themselves with the self-assurance of wealth. They looked at everything around them as if they never doubted their right or ability to own whatever struck their fancy.

Very few guests bothered to speak to her.

She felt uncomfortable and out of place in their company. But Christopher seemed in his element. She watched him circulate through the room, laughing with friends, ignoring her most of the evening.

There was, she noticed, a lot of money passing between hands. Most of it going to Christopher. Undoubtedly to cover bets made on the game. The gleam in his eyes reminded her of her father after a rare lucky day at the track.

At last she could stand no more. Jennifer rushed out through French doors into a formal garden.

Of course, she mused bitterly, he had brought her here to make a point. Christopher Smythe had never considered a lasting friendship with her. He was an aristocrat who had palled around with royals and the children of the rich all of his life. She was an American woman who worked for a living. For a few days she had amused him. But as soon as he had succeeded in charming her into bed, the fascination ended.

Jennifer sat on a chilly stone bench surrounded by late-blooming roses and sighed at the sunset. *The sooner I get home the better,* she thought sadly.

"All alone then, are we?" a refined voice asked.

She turned on the bench and looked up into the gentle brown eyes of one of the men who had played polo that day. His hair was a silvery white, and if she hadn't seen him riding with such amazing agility that day, she might have guessed he was close to seventy years old. He still might be, she thought now, observing the mature lines of his face, but he was as fit as most thirty-year-olds. He had nearly beaten Christopher out of two of his goals.

"For the moment," she said, "yes, I am."

"I'm Richard Crown. I saw you on the field today. You came with Christopher Smythe?"

She smiled, surprised that he had even noticed her in the middle of the frenzied play. But then, she supposed these were small and exclusive social circles, and the aristocracy kept close watch on one another.

"Yes. It was a very exciting match. I'm Jennifer Murphy."

He cocked his head at her non-British accent and frowned softly at her. "You're an American. And very different from Christopher's usual dates. Much nicer, actually."

She noticed he didn't say anything about her being prettier.

Crown seemed to consider his next words more carefully. "Are you living in England…or just visiting?"

"I'm flying back home to the States tomorrow."

"I'm very sorry to hear that. Christopher could use some permanency in his life, a strong and supportive companion."

A resonant voice came out of the shadows. "What Christopher does or doesn't need isn't up for debate."

Jennifer swung around to see Christopher standing at the path's opening. He was glowering darkly at them.

Crown gave him a polite nod. "Fine match today, my boy. That check I owe you will be in tomorrow's mail." He turned back to her. "Goodbye now, Jennifer. It was nice to meet you. I should return to the party. I have some business to tend to."

She lifted her hand in a limp wave.

Christopher was watching her intently. "What did he want?"

"We were just chatting. He seems very nice. Who is he? I mean, he gave his name but—" She shrugged. Despite her disappointment with Christopher, she was curious. The man seemed to be the one pleasant person she'd met all day.

"Lord Richard Crown, the duke of Worth. He's a good man. His family has sat in the House of Lords for as long as anyone can remember. Two of his sons were playing today, as well." He gave her the information grudgingly, his voice tight, his attitude bored.

She wasn't about to stand around and feel unwanted any longer. "I'm ready to go," she said. "I have to be up early to pack and get to the airport."

He nodded. "Fine, we can leave by the garden gate. I've already given my thanks to our hostess."

They started walking in silence.

"Well," Jennifer said to fill the awkward void, "you should have no trouble funding your renovations now."

She had seen him thrust a wad of hundred-pound notes into his pocket earlier in the evening, and who knew how many checks for outrageous sums he'd been handed in payment of wagers. If her father had won that sort of money on his gambling, her mother wouldn't have come so close to filing for bankruptcy.

"Do you bet on every match?" she asked.

"Most of them."

"And you win—"

"Most of the time," he answered with a hint of irony in his voice.

She nodded, offering no comment. If she'd learned one lesson from her father, it was that everyone's luck ran out sooner or later.

Five

Baltimore seemed a gray and lonely place after London and Christopher. Jennifer had just finished writing out a refundable check for her troublesome pair on the last tour. As expected the couple had demanded a partial refund. She sorted through a stack of cruise brochures, pausing at each to stare blindly at its brightly colored cover before returning it to the same pile.

"It doesn't look as if you're making much progress," Evelyn Murphy commented from her computer terminal.

"Jet lag." Jennifer sighed.

Evelyn shook her head at her daughter. "After three days!"

"I'm sorry. I guess I'm just...preoccupied."

"Want to tell me who he was?"

"A man I met in—" Jennifer's head shot up, and

she smiled sheepishly at her mother. "Fell right into that one, didn't I?"

Leaning back in her chair, Evelyn picked up the mug of steaming herb tea from her desktop. "So? What's his name and how did you two meet?"

It was no use trying to put her mother off. Evelyn Murphy was a tenacious woman who never let questions go unanswered.

"His name was Christopher, and he—"

How could she put into words all the many confusing things the young earl had been to her for those few delicious days? She certainly couldn't admit to her mother that she'd slept with the man!

"We met south of Edinburgh, on one of the castle tours." She hesitated, overcome by a warm wave of emotion, a reminder of his arms closing around her. "He was a very handsome man. Different from any other I've ever met," she finished softly.

"I see." Evelyn gazed with interest over the rim of her mug. Jennifer had never seen the energetic woman sit so still. "In what way—different?"

"Christopher Smythe has a title—the earl of Winchester. And he lives in a castle." She laughed and felt herself blushing. "It sounds absurd now."

"Smythe," Evelyn repeated thoughtfully. "He's not the one I've read about in that newspaper I sometimes pick up at the grocery story, is he?"

"He might be. Although he has two brothers who are probably every bit as good at attracting the attention of the press. But," Jennifer added quickly, "he's not exactly the playboy they make him out to be. I mean, he's terribly wealthy and very, very handsome and charismatic. But he has a serious side, too."

Evelyn nodded but made no comment.

Jennifer considered telling her about Christopher's daughter but decided that was information he hadn't meant for her to spread around. She searched for other ways to define him. "He was a very *confusing* man." She stared down at a slick brochure she couldn't remember picking up.

"You had a crush on him," her mother guessed.

Jennifer nodded.

"More than a crush?"

Jennifer shrugged. "We spent some time together. He stepped in as local guide. He knew amazing things about Britain. The group loved him."

"*The group* did, did they?"

Jennifer rolled her eyes. "Don't go reading more into this than there is, Mother. I just sort of…sort of miss his company. He was different and interesting and—"

"And he got under your skin, didn't he?"

In a manner of speaking, Jennifer thought, feeling a bit wicked for the thought. "Chris was fun to be with. But he's too much like Daddy," she said flatly. And that was the heart of it, as far as she could see.

Yes, he had a gentle and loving side when it came to his daughter. But hadn't her own father doted on her in much the same way? And he had let her down, repeatedly.

Her mother put down her tea and stood up to walk across the room toward her. "Are you sure you're not just gun shy? You've never had much of a social life. All men aren't like your father. There are kind, generous, honest men who would do anything to protect their families."

"Instead of doing anything *to* them?" The bitter words came of their own volition. She sighed.

"Daddy was horrid to you. How could you let him take such advantage of you?"

Evelyn shrugged, her face softening for a telltale moment before returning to its determined expression. "I loved him, so I suppose I let him use me. At least, for a time. Listen—" she touched Jennifer affectionately on the arm "—our early years together were wonderful. So exciting. And he gave me you. I'll never regret that."

"But you should have seen through him sooner," Jennifer objected.

"Perhaps. Maybe I thought he would change. But people don't, you know. They are what they are. And your father loved women and had a weakness for horses."

"That's so selfish and cruel," Jennifer stated.

"Selfish, yes. But, as strange as it sounds, I don't believe he ever wanted to hurt either me or you."

Jennifer dropped her head into her hands. Even now, knowing what she did about Christopher—his rich and careless lifestyle, his penchant for brief affairs like the one she'd shared with him—she couldn't hate him. Even now a glow spread through her at the thought of him.

He had touched her, in more than physical ways. She wondered how long it would be before the yearning for him left and she found peace.

Lord Smythe was in the stables again before the sun had fully risen. His sleepy-eyed grooms viewed him dismally over their morning coffee. Before that summer they hadn't needed to rush to their morning chores, as their boss never appeared in the yard before ten in the morning. These days he sometimes rode out in the gray light of dawn.

He always asked for Prince's Pride, his favorite. Fifteen minutes later the pair would be racing across gully and tor, the stallion straining to respond to his master's urgent heels at his belly, sweat running down the man's face and the horse's muscled flanks. Two hours later Christopher would return the exhausted animal to his senior groom.

This morning Jamie eyed both of them with concern. "If ya dunna ruin yerself, sir, yer sure ta ruin the horse." His brogue seemed thicker for his worry. "Nothin's worth doin' in a fine animal like this." He fondly stroked the horse's frothing muzzle.

Christopher gave him an apologetic smile. "I'll be gentler next time."

He walked back toward the castle, his heart no lighter than when he had begun his ride. The day promised to be no better than any other since he and Jennifer had parted in London.

No other woman ever had affected him this deeply, and that vexed him. In the month since he'd last seen Jennifer, he felt like a school lad, suffering through his first infatuation. He couldn't stop thinking about the way she had tipped her head just a little to one side when listening to him describe a long-ago battle. He imagined he smelled vanilla everywhere.

And her body. All the saints and victorious Smythe ancestors protect him! He would give a fortune for one more night in her arms.

But that was impossible. To give in to this strange obsession with her and follow the woman halfway around the world. He just wouldn't do it!

Christopher gazed out across opalescent mists rolling over the loch as he strode toward the house. Between mysteriously shifting vapors, he thought he glimpsed a stubby, red van. He stopped in his tracks, stared, his pulse quickening. Almost immediately the vision was gone.

Last night her voice had come softly to him in his sleep. He had actually reached for her across the sheets.

Suddenly Christopher knew he couldn't stay another hour at Donan. Her presence was everywhere. As soon as he had showered and dressed, he drove to Lisa's school. As he left the administrative office, he saw her trooping with her class and teacher toward the library, chattering gleefully. He took the long way around the parking lot to intercept them.

"Good afternoon, Lord Smythe," the teacher greeted him politely.

He smiled and nodded politely at the woman.

Lisa beamed at him as the line of girls approached. "Hi, Uncle Chris," she chirped as they passed him by. "Are you coming down to London for dinner soon?"

"Soon," he said. "I promise."

"I have a new doll in my collection," she tossed cheerfully back at him.

"Can't wait to see it." The lump in his throat made it impossible to say anything more. He was grateful that he and Lisa had such an easygoing relationship. But it hurt that he couldn't rush over to her and embrace her.

Neither could he whisk her off to Donan with him for a weekend or take her off campus for a lunch in town like other fathers did with their daughters. That would require a call to her mother for special per-

ARTS
GAME

OURSELF IN...

Play **LUCK**

when you play
...then continu
with a sweeth

1. Play Lucky Hearts as instruc

2. Send back this card and you
   books have a cover price of
   are yours to keep absolutely

3. There's no catch! You're und
   ZERO—for your first shipme
   of purchases—not even one

4. The fact is thousands of read
   Reader Service™. They enjoy
   the best new novels at disco
   love their *Heart to Heart* sub
   recipes, book reviews and m

5. We hope that after receiving
   choice is yours—to continu
   invitation, with no risk of an

- ◆ **Exciting Silhouette® romance novels—FREE!**
- ◆ **Plus an exciting mystery gift—FREE!**
- ◆ **No cost! No obligation to buy!**

YES!

I have scratched off the silver card. Please send me the 2 FREE books and gift for which I qualify.
I understand I am under no obligation to purchase any books, as explained on the back and on the opposite page.

With a coin, scratch off the silver card and check below to see what we have for you.

SILHOUETTE'S

LUCKY HEARTS GAME

326 SDL C6N3

225 SDL C6NX
(S-D-OS-01/01)

| | | | | | | | | | | | | | | | | | | |

NAME   (PLEASE PRINT CLEARLY)

| | | | | | | | | | | | | | | | | | | |

ADDRESS

| | | | | | | | | | | | | | | | | | | |

APT.#   CITY

| | | | | | | | | | | | | | | | | | | |

STATE/PROV.   ZIP/POSTAL CODE

Twenty-one gets you 2 free books, and a free mystery gift!

Twenty gets you 2 free books!

Nineteen gets you 1 free book!

Try Again!

Offer limited to one per household and not valid to current Silhouette Desire® subscribers. All orders subject to approval.

The Silhouette Reader Service™—Here's how it works:

Accepting your 2 free books and gift places you under no obligation to buy anything. You may keep the books and gift and return the shipping statement marked "cancel." If you do not cancel, about a month later we'll send you 6 additional novels and bill you just $3.34 each in the U.S., or $3.74 each in Canada, plus 25¢ shipping & handling per book and applicable taxes if any.* That's the complete price and — compared to cover prices of $3.99 each in the U.S. and $4.50 each in Canada — it's quite a bargain! You may cancel at any time, but if you choose to continue, every month we'll send you 6 more books, which you may either purchase at the discount price or return to us and cancel your subscription.

*Terms and prices subject to change without notice. Sales tax applicable in N.Y. Canadian residents will be charged applicable provincial taxes and GST.

mission. And he had absolutely no say in her future. Where she would go to college...what sort of career she might pursue...who her friends would be and who she might eventually marry.

For the thousandth time he wished with all his soul that he hadn't promised Sandra to keep their secret. But he was nothing if not a man of his word.

Besides, as more time passed, the situation became more rather than less complicated. Lisa had grown up knowing him as "Uncle Chris." She had started calling him that before she could pronounce Christopher or Lord Smythe, or most any other word. What would happen to their warm friendship if she suddenly learned he had been hiding the truth from her all these years? He couldn't bear to think of her disillusionment.

That evening when he eventually returned to Donan, there was a letter waiting for him, postmarked London. He recognized Sir Isaac's coat of arms. Perhaps, he thought, with a burst of anticipatory joy, this was the message he had been waiting for. Christopher ripped open the envelope and pulled out a single sheet of vellum.

He read rapidly, out of breath from the first word, but as the meaning sank in, his heart sank, too. The letter was from Lisa's mother, not Sir Isaac. It didn't release him from keeping his secret. Sandra was taking Lisa to the south of France on holiday for two weeks. He would be without even a glimpse of his daughter for at least fifteen days...half a month.

He felt desolate as he dropped the letter on the marble-topped console and stomped away. Sadness gave way to anger at the lack of control he had over his own life and the lives of the people he wanted to keep close to him. Damn holidays! Damn the female sex for having such a hold on him!

As his foot hit the bottom step, he looked up the curving staircase that Jennifer had climbed with him. Her sweet face flashed before him, and along with it came a sudden, wonderful jolt of inspiration.

"Go ahead and take a long lunch," Jennifer told her mother. "I'm not very hungry, anyway, and business is slow today."

Evelyn observed her daughter for a moment. "You haven't eaten enough to keep a hummingbird alive in weeks. How about I bring you back a nice, hearty sausage sub from Gino's? Loads of spicy meat, his marvelous Italian sauce, grilled green peppers and onions and a thick slice of mozzarella cheese melted on top."

"Sounds like an invitation to a coronary," Jennifer mumbled.

"But you'll die happy. You're sure?" she asked, gently.

"No, thanks. Really," Jennifer said. "I brought a salad. I'll be better off with that."

Her mother turned away, but stopped with her hand on the doorknob and stared through the glass pane. "Oh, my."

"What?" Jennifer asked. Either there was another bad traffic accident on Charles Street or her mother had spotted a dress she envied.

"Will you look at *that*. Now if *he* couldn't make a nun break her vows!"

"Mother, will you stop ogling men. That's what gets us women into trouble. They're like chocolates. They're never as good as they look."

Evelyn sighed. "This one might be. Oh, dear...oh, no, he...he's coming this way!"

Jennifer laughed as her mother leaped back from the door and practically dived behind her desk. She was sitting demurely behind it when the stranger rushed open the door and the little brass bell over it tinkled in welcome.

"May I help y—" Jennifer choked over the last word and stared in disbelief at the tall, elegantly dressed man who stepped into Murphy's Worldwide Escapes. "Chris?"

He looked at her for just a moment before glancing around the office to see she was not alone. "I decided to take you up on your offer, Miss Murphy." His voice was low and rumbled pleasantly within her.

She swallowed. "Offer?"

Her mind went blank. But she could imagine a dozen things she *might* have offered Christopher Smythe in the heat of the moment. None of which was pronounceable with her mother in the room.

"I...I, well, yes. Of course." Out of habit she waved a hand toward the customer's seat on the other side of her desk. He stepped forward. Thankfully her brain began to function again. "A tour of Baltimore!" she cried out triumphantly.

Her mother gave her a puzzled look, then recognition flooded her features and Jennifer knew she realized who it was.

Christopher ignored the chair. Instead, he strode directly to Evelyn's cubicle.

"You must be Jennifer's mother. The resemblance is striking." He held out his hand to her. When she slowly reached out as if to shake hands with him, he drew her fingertips briefly to his lips. "Lovely." He smiled at her, his blue eyes sparkling.

Evelyn blushed. "Oh, my." She shot an approving smile at her daughter. "Would I be wrong in guessing this is your earl?"

Jennifer opened her mouth to answer, but he beat her to it.

"Christopher Smythe, pleased to meet you. Has Jennifer told you all about us?"

Jennifer flinched. *All!* She shot him a horrified expression. His eyes darkened and seemed to laugh at her discomfort.

"Jennifer told me," her mother began cautiously, "that you two met and spent a few days *touring* together. Although…she sometimes has a habit of understating things." Evelyn winked at him.

Good grief, Jennifer thought, *she's flirting with him!*

She shot up out of her chair. "Mother, why don't you head on out for lunch. You need a break, and I'll take care of things here." She needed to know why Christopher was here. Although she couldn't believe it had anything to do with her, she didn't want witnesses around to see the look of disappointment on her face when he confirmed that.

"I have a better idea," he said. "I'll take both of you out for lunch, or for dinner if the first isn't possible."

Evelyn glowed. "Oh, that is very nice of you," she said, then produced a soap-opera frown. "But I'm afraid both of us can't leave at the same time. We're terribly busy today."

Jennifer stared suspiciously at her mother. Not a

half dozen people had walked through the door all morning!

"That's too bad," Christopher said. "Perhaps dinner?"

Evelyn pouted. "I'm sorry. I have plans for the evening."

Jennifer's eyes narrowed another notch. The grandest plans her mother ever had involved a night of bridge at her friend Bertha's house.

Christopher turned back to Jennifer. "Then I guess it's just you and me, luv."

"But I can't leave my mother here without—"

"I'm fine, I'm fine. You two run along. I have *my salad* for lunch." She shot Jennifer a knowing look.

Jennifer sighed. The two of them had never met before, and already they were plotting against her. "Just let me get my jacket," she muttered.

They walked down Charles Street toward the waterfront. The fall air was crisp and pleasant. Store windows displayed pumpkins and Indian corn. At last Jennifer worked up the nerve to speak.

"Why are you here?"

"Business," Christopher replied quickly.

"Really?"

He rolled his eyes thoughtfully. "I suppose that might be stretching the truth. At first it was a matter of providence. Sandra notified me that she was taking Lisa out of the country, and I felt at loose ends."

"I see."

"I started thinking that I hadn't taken a holiday in years."

"And you work so hard that you needed a break from castle life," she commented dryly.

"Don't be a smart aleck, it doesn't suit you."

"Then why?"

"I felt like a cad for playing the role of aristocrat to your Eliza Doolittle," he admitted. "I was showing off, taking you to a polo match and party where I knew the crowd would be a snooty one. I wanted you to be put off. I was wrong to do that."

"You were merely demonstrating the differences between us. I was convinced and left for home."

"I don't think a title and money really matter when it comes to—" He struggled for the right words.

"Affairs of the heart?"

"Yes. When it comes to whatever draws a man and a woman together." His eyes were intensely blue, demanding that she not turn away.

They crossed Charles Street, then Light Street and walked in silence along the row of chic restaurants and boutiques circling the harbor. Jennifer thought nothing of the sights, but she was aware of Christopher's every move. His arm slipped warmly around her waist as they walked. She stepped sideways and out of his reach. Her mind whirled with a hundred doubts. What did he want from her?

"It hurt when you made so little of what happened between us," she whispered, just loud enough for him to hear above city noises.

"It was wrong of me. I'm sorry."

She took deep breaths of the moist air, trying to unravel her own emotions while figuring out his. "So you flew to America to apologize for being a jerk?"

He smiled down at her. "Something like that. Maybe more."

"To take me out to dinner as penance?"

"More." He was smiling broadly now.

She frowned suspiciously up at him.

He took a quick sidestep, coiled his arm around her a second time and brought her firmly against his hip to prevent her from escaping. She was vividly reminded of the intimacy they had shared.

"I won't sleep with you again," she stated decisively.

"I have no intention of asking for a second one-night stand."

"By definition, that's impossible." She felt just a little smug. If she was able to banter with him, even though her entire nervous system was in chaos, maybe it was going to be okay!

"I want us to find a way to be together," he said.

Jennifer stopped walking. She stared up at Christopher in disbelief. "You can't be serious."

"I am. Totally. You're a fascinating and beautiful woman, Jenny. I can't stop thinking about you."

She turned away from him to look out across the harbor. A seagull landed a few feet away and eyed them hopefully before deciding their intent wasn't to feed him.

"You're just saying that because I'm a challenge. The distance, geographically. The distance between us socially. I'm not like your other women, so I'm—" She shrugged, feeling muddled, dizzy. "I don't know what I am to you. An appealing oddity?"

"No!" he snapped. Gripping her shoulders, he turned her to face him. "Tell me the name of the best restaurant in this city. I'll take you to lunch and we'll talk. Just please hear me out."

She didn't answer him. She couldn't.

"Jennifer, I've come all this way, and I've told you I don't often leave my little island. You can at least allow me to say my piece."

Every instinct shouted at her to run like hell. She had suffered heartbreak once, and that had come after being with him for only a few days and sleeping with him once. What excruciating level of pain would she be letting herself in for if she committed herself to a real relationship with the earl of Winchester?

"Hamptons, the dining room at the Harbor Court Hotel." She made a face at him. "You're the only person I actually know who can afford to eat there. But anything you say won't make a difference."

He laughed. "Ah—I love a challenge!"

His lightheartedness was a pretense, but he hoped she wouldn't see through it. In the anxious moments before he had walked into the travel agency, he had feared immediate rejection. Even now, as they walked into the hotel, he wondered if the trip had been pointless. What if he bared his soul to her and she still turned him down?

They were seated by the maître d' at a window overlooking the harbor. After the sommelier had brought a crisp Chardonnay to their table, Christopher plunged in.

"You already know my reasons for staying in Britain. Because of Lisa, I can't live anywhere else."

"I know that," she said softly, sipping her wine.

"And this is your home and where your business is."

"You made that point some time ago, on another continent."

She wasn't making this easy on him, but he didn't blame her. Admittedly, he had treated her badly. Christopher leaned across the table. "Jennifer, I'm trying to say that I want you in my life, although making that happen won't be easy."

Her pale-green eyes turned a watery gray. "I'm not sure that's what I want."

He was stunned. "You don't feel that we have something special?"

"I didn't say that. I'm just not convinced that pursuing a relationship now would be worth the risk for either of us."

He reached for her fingertips and held on when he sensed she might pull away. "I don't understand. Are you afraid I'll want out again?"

She lifted her chin and looked him directly in the eyes. "Not immediately, but yes…eventually."

"How can you know that?"

"Because your whole life revolves around wealth, pursuing it and protecting it." She desperately wanted him to understand. "I saw you enthusiastically collecting your winnings after the polo match. As much money as you already have, you were thrilled to be raking in more."

"But it wasn't for—"

"No, let me finish," she insisted, emotions bubbling within her she couldn't hold back. "You don't know me, Chris. You can't understand how disturbing seeing you like that was for me. My father chased pretty women and gambled away every penny he could get his hands on. He could have chosen a good, honest life with me and my mother. Instead he risked everything on his vices."

Christopher frowned. "You believe we're of the same ilk?"

Solemnly she nodded. "I remember how charming Daddy could be. I remember the way my mother looked at him—her eyes full of him. She was devoted to the man, heart and soul. When I'm around you, I feel the way she looked.''

Jennifer sat back in her chair, pulling her fingertips free of his. She forced herself to take slow, calming breaths.

''And that's the only reason you won't consider being with me?''

She lifted one shoulder in a gesture of concurrence. ''Isn't that enough?''

''Don't you ever look beneath the surface of a person?'' Christopher demanded in a low, angry voice. He didn't like being misjudged. He might not have always been an angel. Lisa was living proof. But he wasn't as bad as she imagined.

''Of course I do!'' she objected with a huff.

''If a prospective client can't afford luxury accommodations, you don't refuse to do business with him. Right?''

''Right.''

''Then why discriminate against a man born to money?''

''It's not the being *born* to it that matters,'' she argued.

''What then?''

''Well, you don't work at all. You play rich men's games and tinker with a castle.''

''I spend a good thirty or more hours out of every week administering my daughter's school, raising funds for it and for other schools that take in indigent children.''

She frowned at him. ''You do?''

''Remember the wagers I was collecting at the party?''

''Yes,'' she admitted hesitantly.

"I always bet on the outcome of my polo matches. I work bloody hard to win because the stakes are high. If my team does win, the losers make their checks out to one of the schools I support. If we lose, I have to postpone some of my restoration projects at Donan."

Her eyes widened at that. "Oh." She looked away from him, nibbling pensively at her lower lip.

Good, he thought, she was beginning to understand at least a little of what made him tick.

"The castle isn't a game for me," he continued with feeling. "I've already told you my plans for it. If I can pull off all the necessary repairs, I'll present Donan as a gift to the people of Scotland, as a memorial to those who gave their lives defending her."

Jennifer thought how much more complex this man was than she had ever guessed. He cherished the daughter he was being kept by a pledge from claiming. He cared about other children, too—the poor as well as the rich. He felt deeply about his own ancestors and even their enemies. He chose to honor all he loved in very special ways.

He was kind and good, sexy and strong, and he made her want to surrender to him on the spot. If ever a man had given her reason to love him, Christopher was that man. "Maybe I've been too hasty," she whispered. "Let's talk some more. I can't make any decisions tonight."

He smiled, satisfied for at least that much, and laid his hand over hers on the table. She felt a reminiscent ripple of heat run up her arm. How she had missed his amazing body and the pleasures he was capable of giving her.

"I trust you, Jennifer. Now let me prove I can be trusted," he said.

Trust.

The familiar fear stabbed at her heart. Would she ever be able to completely trust her happiness to any man? Just a few months ago her answer would have been an immediate and resounding, *No!* But being this close to Christopher and having learned so many good things about him...she couldn't turn him down without time to think.

Six

Christopher had been in Baltimore five days, and Jennifer still hadn't given him her answer.

They had shared a romantic Spanish dinner at Tio Pepe's, continental cuisine at the uptown Brass Elephant and had topped off a sumptuous Neapolitan feast in Little Italy with cappuccino. They had talked endlessly of plans for restoring his beloved Castle Donan. He felt closer to Jennifer with every passing day. But they had not slept together again.

Each night he returned to his hotel suite after escorting her back to her apartment. He sat alone, staring at white pinpoints of city lights encircling the harbor, trying to be patient while fearing he was losing her. What more could he offer than the friendship, admiration and physical joys they'd already shared?

If she was holding out for marriage…that was out of the question. No woman had ever kept his attention for more than a handful of months. Jennifer was special, but he couldn't believe that in the end, she would turn out to be different from the others. Besides, in her heart of hearts she was still convinced that he would turn out like her father—a womanizing wastrel who would leave her penniless.

On Friday evening he was to pick her up at her place. They had tickets to the symphony. But he felt too edgy to sit through a concert. He wanted her so badly he ached, but he refused to press her to sleep with him. His only hope was that she would choose a plain dress and look terribly unappealing tonight.

Christopher knocked on her door. There was no answer. After trying again he heard a subtle change in the sounds coming from her apartment. The shower shutting off? He glanced at his watch; he was fifteen minutes early. Footsteps padded across the tile floor behind the door.

"Chris? Is that you?"

"Yes." He stuffed his hands in his pockets to keep them still. He wanted to reach through the door and grab her. "Sorry," he mumbled. "Running a little early, I guess."

"No problem." A latch clicked open, and she flung open the door. "I'll be ready in a jiffy."

Stepping inside, he was in time to see her towel-wrapped body skitter around the corner out of the living room. All the requisite territory was covered, yet he had never witnessed a more provocative sight. The fullness of her bottom beneath plush terry cloth. A bare curve of pale shoulders above the towel's upper edge. Her hair hung damp, brushed smooth down the slim nape of her neck.

"Please," he muttered shakily, "give me strength."

"What did you say?" she called from the bedroom.

"Nothing." Christopher couldn't sit down, couldn't put a coherent thought next to another. He paced her living room, reminding himself of all the reasons he shouldn't take one step closer to the bedroom.

He glanced nervously toward the door. She'd swung it closed as she passed through. But it had eased itself open a few inches. Through the crack he glimpsed a slice of jade-green carpeting, one corner of a dark wooden chest of drawers, part of a mirror reflecting the image of a closet.

He jerked away, chiding himself for being so weak. A gentleman wouldn't look a second time. But— bloody hell!—he wasn't feeling very gentlemanly at the moment. He was hot, extremely aroused, in dire *need!*

Christopher planted himself firmly in the middle of the living room, his back to Jennifer's bedroom door.

But his eyes betrayed him, drifting over his shoulder as if pulled by a powerful magnet. A trickle of sweat ran hotly beneath his collar. He could hear her moving about, but couldn't see her. Perhaps she was fully dressed by now?

Yes, she would be. Almost certainly. He was going to make it! He wouldn't make a fool of himself or embarrass her by storming her bedroom door.

Then he caught his breath. For, suddenly, there she was, poised in front of her closet in a sleeveless red dress. A band of fabric wound up over Jennifer's slim shoulders, looping behind her slim neck as she stood with her back to him. The skirt fell in soft folds around her long legs.

She was so pretty, yet utterly unaware. She stole the breath right out of him. He couldn't tear his eyes away from her, even when she impulsively unzipped her dress and stepped out of it.

All she wore beneath it were lacy bikini panties. No bra. No slip. Now he couldn't look away, no matter how hard he tried.

She pulled a little black dress from the closet and held it up to her body, turning toward the mirror. One side of her breast, a single darkly pigmented nipple, and the smooth curve of waist reflected back to him. Christopher swung away from the delectable image with excruciating effort, staggered toward the living room window and crashed into her coffee table. The chrome legs screeched in protest across the wood floor.

"What happened? Are you all right?" Jennifer called from the other room.

"Fine. I'm just fine," he grumbled, gathering himself up and repositioning the table.

He looked back toward her door. It was fully shut now. He winced. What a clumsy toad he had been. She must have guessed by now that he'd been ogling her.

Minutes later Jennifer stepped coolly into the living room. Enough time should have passed for him to regain his composure. But his flesh felt prickly with urgency. His arousal hadn't lessened now that she was decently clothed.

He met her eyes and knew he couldn't pretend innocence. "I'm sorry."

"What have you got to be sorry for?" she asked. But a faint blush colored her cheeks.

"You realize I was watching you...um, well... change your mind about the dress."

She smiled and shrugged. "That's my fault, I should have closed the door all the way."

"I didn't intend to spy on you. I'm not a voyeur, it just happened. I looked around and there you were," he said in his own defense. It was almost true.

"If it had been the other way around—you had been changing and I was cooling my heels in the living room—maybe I would be the one apologizing," she suggested playfully. Her eyes twinkled.

It struck him without warning that she might actually have *known* he was watching her, and that she had been as excited as he was. But the other idea, that *she* might enjoy clandestinely observing *him*, sans clothing, was even more intriguing.

"I'll remember that," he said, meaning it. "Anytime you want me to strip for you, just say the word."

Her expression shifted subtly. She ran the tip of her tongue delicately across her top lip and looked away.

"What is it, Jenny?"

Blinking up at him, she clasped her hands in front of her. "I don't think I'm in the mood for the symphony tonight."

"Ah," he said, his body heat intensifying with a sudden blast, as if someone had thrown another log on the fire. His voice dropped an octave. "What *are* you in the mood for?"

"The same thing I've thought about ever since I left London," she whispered. "Wanting to make love with you again might not be wise, but it's what I want...what I *need*."

Her words made his body tighten with anticipation. "But you're still afraid," he guessed.

"Yes, of losing you."

"You won't."

She gritted her teeth and forced her next words through them, her eyes flashing. "Don't promise me something you can't be sure of yourself."

"I don't break promises."

No, she thought, *not when they affect your daughter. But what about where women are concerned?*

How could she be sure he hadn't promised a tomorrow to other lovers? How could she be sure he hadn't meant to be faithful, then had fallen out of love or lust or whatever it was that men felt when attracted to a woman?

"We can't be together for long," she reminded him. "You have to return to Scotland, for Lisa and for Donan."

"Come with me." The words were out of his mouth before he felt his lips move. But once suspended in the emotion-charged air between them, they sounded right. *Come with me and be my love.* Yes, if he could only make her see that it was the right thing to do. "Come to Scotland with me," he repeated, his voice suddenly firm.

Jennifer stared up at him, her lips gently parted, quivering.

He didn't want to consider the immense changes that would be forced on her life if she took him up on his proposition. Frankly, he didn't care. All that mattered was possessing her any way he could, for as long as he could. If asking her to come live with him at the castle was what it took—so be it.

Jennifer didn't know why she was even considering

his proposal seriously, but she was. Being with Christopher for the past five days had been heaven and hell woven into one heady experience. She had longed for his touch, yet feared the inevitable moment when he would try again to seduce her...and she must refuse him. She had yearned for his kisses, but found ways to avoid them. The torment had been unbearable.

All of her life she had behaved reasonably. She had dismissed long shots, risk, instability and passionate flings. She had vowed she would never fall into the trap of loving a man who loved women, horses and his own freedom too much.

Yet here was temptation in the flesh, gazing at her with those wonderful deep-blue eyes, offering her a life of luxury and romance in a country far away.

And she was seriously considering accepting.

"You must have known when I followed you here that I wasn't going to leave without you," he murmured, stepping closer to her.

Had he subconsciously known it, too? *Yes,* Christopher thought. He reached out for her limp hand and traced the fine lines in her palm with his fingertip.

"No...yes...well maybe I did," she murmured feeling utterly confused.

"I understand your fears, Jenny. I won't let you down like your father did. I promise."

"It's not that I don't believe you, it's just that I don't—" She broke off, unable to finish.

"Trust me?" he supplied. "It's not the same thing, is it? Believing and trusting. Maybe trust is something a man has to earn. But if you don't give me a chance, how can I prove myself?"

He brought her fingertips to his lips, kissed them

gently, then drew her toward him, wrapping his strong arms around her.

When she turned her face up at him, he lowered his head and kissed her on the mouth. It was a long time before either took a breath.

"Well?" he asked

"But Scotland," she breathed, her eyes wide.

"Don't tell me you'd be satisfied with a commuter relationship." He held her tighter. "Because I know I never would be. I want you in my bed, woman…not thousands of miles away."

Her heart raced as his warm lips covered hers once more. Her head clouded, spun and she felt a steamy need to be touched as he had touched her before. Then, in London, they had had only two days. The extravagance of having Christopher to herself for weeks, months, possibly even years…was a temptation too delicious to let pass.

"Chris," she murmured.

Beneath the pleading tone of her voice was all the answer he needed.

His hands moved to the zipper of her dress. "I liked the red one better," he whispered huskily in her ear, making her shudder delightfully.

"I'm not particularly fond of what you're wearing, either," she retaliated shyly, then tugged loose his striped tie and tossed it aside.

"The red dress didn't require a bra or slip," he pointed out, moving a strap off her shoulder to reveal two more narrow bands of fabric. "Much more economical, materially speaking."

She laughed, her eyes dancing at the game. "Men and their suits. Boring standard gear. I could do without them entirely."

She yanked off his jacket, then plucked free the tails of his dress shirt and began to unbutton it. Beneath the smooth, white silk, his chest was bare. She loved looking at him—dark male fur, muscles standing out in rigid definition. She combed her trembling fingers through the short, black curls.

He had her slip off now and was unclasping her bra. Jennifer closed her eyes as he drew the lacy cups down her arms and off. She stood before him and let him take his time inspecting her.

Feeling his eyes drift over her was both thrilling and terrifying. She sensed his pleasure with her, but feared living up to his expectations. Being with a man once was one thing—the novelty of a new lover being such a potent aphrodisiac. But how would she ever hold his interest past a second time...a tenth...a hundredth?

Christopher suddenly demanded all of *her* attention as his mouth covered hers and his hand pressed over her breast. He wrapped his arm around her bare waist and walked her backward to the sofa, easing her down onto the cool cushions.

"I have great plans for you." His voice was playfully gruff.

"Oh?"

His kisses descended her throat to her breasts. She shivered at the moist flicks of his tongue over her nipples, gazed down into his rich eyes. He looked up at her from between her flushed breasts, his eyes sparkling with mischief as he drew the tip of one nipple between his lips and teeth.

She let out a delighted yip, threw her head back and arched toward him. "You're wicked."

"Yes," he agreed. "And about to become more so, luv."

A wave of heat coursed through her. A second followed, setting her writhing as she felt his wide palm smooth down across her hip and behind to cup her bottom and press her hips against his. He was hard and ready, although still clothed below the waist. It seemed all the more exciting, her being totally naked while he still hadn't fully revealed himself to her.

"In my pocket," he whispered as his mouth continued to work its magic—kissing, teasing, possessing her breasts, one then the other, until she felt herself grow moist and tingle deliciously.

"Your pocket?" she repeated, at a loss.

"I can't wait much longer, luv."

"Oh!" Jennifer's fingers edged into the warm fold of fabric at his hip and came out with the necessary item.

"You do it," he said.

Shakily she tore open the tiny packet as Christopher shifted his weight off to one side and unzipped his pants. She could hardly breathe, hardly make her fingers function. He seemed to enjoy her difficulty concentrating on the task while he distracted her with kisses and caresses.

At last he eased his pants and briefs off the rest of the way and knelt over her to make things easier.

She looked at him. Really looked at him from close up for the first time. He was full, long, steely hard and very beautiful in the most masculine of ways.

Jennifer let her fingers linger on him as she completed her job. A pulsing sensation moved low within her body, as if she could already feel how it would be when he entered her. Looking up, she saw in his face a hunger that matched her own. For these amazing moments, she was all he wanted—just as he was everything to her.

Jennifer lay down, stretching her toes toward the far end of the couch, her arms up over her head, inviting him to come to her with every inch of her body.

He waited, his eyes drifting over her. She liked the way he fought his hunger. At last he seized a small throw pillow from the end of the sofa and slid it beneath her hips. She looked up at him, puzzled for a few seconds before he lowered his head and drew his tongue quickly down her tummy, across her navel, wandering lower still.

She let out a faint whimper of surprise as his kisses burrowed into her soft feminine nest. She looked down at him, glorying in the new sensations he was giving her, loving the way his eyes flamed knowingly up at her. As if he instinctively knew that what he was about to do for her was something no man before him had dared.

Gently parting her long limbs, he found her feminine core with the tip of his tongue. Jennifer shuddered and pressed herself up from the pillow to more fully meet his mouth. Waves of flame swirled round her, lifting her higher, higher still, until all around her seemed consumed in a glorious red haze. And she cried out in ecstasy.

But Christopher didn't stop or take his own gratification yet.

It was as if he could read the mounting curve of her passion, as if he knew better than she what she needed. His generous mouth and wickedly clever fingers coaxed another and still another delicious climax from her body, until she was gasping his name. At last she fell limp with exhaustion against the couch cushions, her body humming contentedly.

"I believe it's now my turn, m'lady," she heard him whisper huskily from above her. Smiling up at him, she opened herself to him.

Christopher plunged into her with a possessive fury.

He thrust only a few times before he let out a lusty groan of male satisfaction and collapsed over her, breathing heavily, tasting her lips one last time before resting his own against her perspiring throat.

Jennifer wrapped her arms around him, cherishing the delicious afterglow of their lovemaking as she drifted off to sleep beneath him.

Seven

Jennifer left Christopher in her bed the next morning. She ached to stay with him, warm and safe in his arms, reassured by his sleeping presence. But even after a week's preparations, there was so much to be done before she could leave with him for Scotland.

As she stood in the cozy office where she had, as a child, done her homework while her mother worked, then later joined Evelyn to run the business, she looked fondly around the brilliantly postered walls. Scenes of exotic lands and ads for ski and cruise holidays reminded her of the fascinating places she'd shared with her customers over the years. The computer terminals, three lines on the phones, and stacks of mail also brought back the hard work that had gone into building Murphy's Worldwide Escapes into a modest success.

Was she throwing all of this away on a dream that

might end up a heartbreaking nightmare? A heavy knot bunched in her stomach and, although she took several slow, deep breaths, they didn't relieve the tension building inside of her.

Gently a hand patted her arm. "He'll be here to take you to the airport in just a few hours, dear. Don't you think you had better finish cleaning out your desk?"

Jennifer swung around in desperation to face her mother. "Tell me I'm doing the right thing."

Evelyn smiled. "Do you love him?"

How many times had Jennifer asked herself that same question? It had never resulted in a satisfactory answer. All she felt now was a disturbing wave of nausea. "I think I must. I wouldn't risk leaving my home and all of this if I didn't."

"Think of it as just another tour," her mother suggested. "The only difference is that you and Christopher are the only travelers."

Jennifer laughed wryly and shook her head. "I don't even know the itinerary, or how long the trip will last."

"A little like the rest of life isn't it?" Evelyn opened her arms to her daughter. They turned the reassuring hug into a shared embrace, comforting to both of them.

When Jennifer pulled away, she felt a little better. "It's just that I feel I'm risking so much, and not all of it is mine to gamble."

Evelyn shook her head. "If you mean that you're somehow endangering *my* future by flying off with your young earl to Scotland, put *that* out of your head. I have a new assistant lined up to cover the office. As soon as she finishes training, I'll be itching to lead tours again. The business will be fine.''

"What about you, Mom?'' Jennifer asked with concern. "Will *you* be all right?''

"I'll miss you, of course. But I won't be able to resist my curiosity for long. One day I'll hop on a jet and come visit the two of you and that castle you've been raving about.'' Evelyn gave her a mysterious smile. "In the meantime, it's not as if I don't have a life of my own. In fact, I have a date next Saturday.''

"A date? With a man? You?'' Jennifer grinned sheepishly. "I mean…not that you're too *old* or anything like that.''

"You'd better believe it, young lady,'' Evelyn said firmly, her eyes bright. "It's about time I stopped looking at half the world's population as the enemy.'' Her expression turned suddenly serious. "Don't let my experience with your father destroy your chances for happiness. Try not to be cynical about love.''

"I will try,'' Jennifer promised.

"Good. Now,'' Evelyn pronounced in her back-to-business voice, "get that desk cleaned out so my new employee will have a place for her things. And remember, if this romantic tour of yours doesn't work out, you'll always have a place to come back to. You won't have lost a thing.''

Jennifer gazed down at her tightly clenched fists. *That's not true,* she thought sadly. For she surely would have lost her heart.

As Christopher drove the Jag up the winding drive to Castle Donan, Jennifer sat forward in the passenger seat and felt her heart swell with delight at the sight of the magnificent stone structure. It seemed as moody and ruggedly beautiful as its master. And she loved the one as much as the other.

"What are you thinking?" he asked when he shut off the engine and she sat unmoving in her seat, gazing up at the turret where they had first kissed.

"How lovely this place will be once all the work has been done."

"Yes," he said. "It will be." But his eyes were fixed on her, not on the ancient fortress. "We have plenty of time for work. It's been a long two days of traveling. Let's unpack, see if Mrs. Clark has left us something for supper, then go off to bed."

She blushed, knowing the smoldering flecks in his eyes meant he would make long, slow love to her high above the misty moors before either of them found sleep that night.

They dined on cold roasted chicken, sliced fresh garden tomatoes sprinkled with olive oil and herbs, thick slabs of crusty oat bread slathered with creamy butter and a delicious selection of cheeses and sliced fruits and berries for dessert. Afterward, full of good food and sleepy from the wine that had accompanied it, Jennifer took the hand Christopher offered and climbed the elegant stone staircase with him to their room.

He paused at each landing to enfold her in his arms and press soft kisses over her closed eyes, her cheeks and throat. And he whispered the same words each time: "Thank you. Thank you for coming with me."

Christopher woke before Jennifer stirred. He turned over between the sheets and watched her sleep, grateful to whatever power had brought her to him. She was pure joy, the happiest thing that had come into

his life in a very long time. Happier, in a way, than
the birth of his daughter, because that had been a
bittersweet time in his life. He hadn't been able to
claim Lisa. But Jennifer was with him, and he intended to keep her for as long as he was able.

Christopher dressed quickly, took the long twist of
stairs in twos and greeted Mrs. Clark who was already
busy in the kitchen. "I'll introduce you to Jennifer
sometime today," he promised. "But I'm sure jet lag
will have the best of her for the morning."

"Don't you go hurryin' your precious betrothed,"
she scolded him. "The lass'll be seein' enough of me
soon. Why don't you take her a tray. She'll wake
famished."

"Good idea," he said, smiling affectionately at the
older woman.

Christopher had had the presence of mind to telephone the Clarks before his flight back to Britain.
Carefully, he had chosen his words, describing Miss
Murphy as a *friend.* He knew only too well that An-
nabelle Clark would give him a hard time if the relationship wasn't made clear from the start.

The call had done no good at all. Although the
woman had always treated his girlfriends cordially,
she had never attached any more permanence to them
than he had. For reasons unfathomable to him, this
time she started calling Jennifer his "betrothed" as
soon as he announced she would be staying at Donan
for an undetermined time.

"Let's start with a carafe of your good coffee," he
said, surrendering.

"And scones with fresh butter, oatmeal and fruit.
From the little I glimpsed of her from our cottage
window last night in the dark, I'd say your intended

is needin' some good, hearty food. Scrawny little thing, she is."

Not where it counts, Christopher nearly replied.

Half an hour later, he took the tray up to the suite at the top of the turret. Jennifer twisted around in bed, pulled the sheets up over her breasts and smiled up at him. They had slept without nightclothes, and she looked just as delectable this morning as she had last night.

He set the tray on the bedside table and kissed her. "Sleep well for your first night?"

"Heavenly," she said with a sigh. Her eyes shifted with interest to the tray. "What's this?"

"Breakfast. I ate in the kitchen. It's all yours."

"Good thing, too. I'm famished." She gasped as she uncovered a steaming bowl of cream-splashed Scottish oatmeal sprinkled with brown sugar. "Oh, this looks marvelous!"

"I wasn't sure you'd like it."

She took a huge spoonful. "I adore hot cereal. Makes me think of being a little girl on a cold winter morning."

He watched with pleasure as she ate. They talked of plans for rejuvenating the gardens and furnishing some of the empty rooms. Jennifer's ideas newly inspired him. He made a mental note to call in a local landscaper to do the heavy work in the garden before the ground froze solid, so that Jennifer could plant spring bulbs.

"Before we go any further with this," he said, snitching a piece of toast, "we should discuss your salary."

She looked up at him and quickly swallowed the coffee in her mouth. "My *what?*"

"Salary. You don't think I expect you to do all of this work for nothing, do you?"

Jennifer put down the heavy ceramic mug on the tray. "To be honest, I didn't expect anything. I agreed to come to Donan because I wanted to be with you. And I like hard work."

"I don't think you understand how much physical labor is involved."

"I understand perfectly," she snapped, hurt by this blatant reminder of their still-undefined relationship.

To her mind they had entered into a very personal kind of partnership. She had no spousal claims on his land, castle or anything he owned…and she didn't care about any of that. But did he actually consider her a *paid employee?*

"What's wrong, Jenny?" He laid a hand over hers.

She shook it off, glaring up at him. "This isn't a *job* to me, Chris."

He frowned. "Well, of course it isn't. But it wouldn't be fair if you came away from this with nothing."

Came away…as if he was already planning for the day when they would part.

"No, it wouldn't," she said distinctly, then bit down on her bottom lip. How shrewish she sounded. This wasn't like her at all, and now he was staring at her with a perplexed look. "I'm sorry," Jennifer murmured. "I guess I saw this venture in a more…à different way than you do."

"I've never moved anyone in my employ into my bedroom."

His eyes twinkled, as if he was wondering when she might figure things out for herself. They were trying to strike a delicate balance in their new relationship; she understood that much. But he always seemed to be three steps ahead of her.

He continued, "I can't in good conscience put you to physical labor and give you nothing in return." He flashed her a smile full of the devil. "Unless we could trade one sort of favor for another."

He hauled her out of the bed as easily as lifting a pillow. She laughed, knowing she'd lost any chance, for the moment, of unscrambling her feelings or understanding his. For better or worse her heart was in his hands as surely as her body was in his arms.

"Who's to say I won't receive those favors without my lifting even a pinky finger," she managed to come back at him playfully.

He put on a thoughtful expression. "How about a compromise?"

"What do you suggest?" she asked warily.

He kissed the tip of her nose. "We'll agree upon a fair fee for your services, which will be sent directly to Evelyn. She can invest it in Murphy's Worldwide Escapes, to your benefit and hers since you each own half. Or she can deposit it in an account for a rainy day, should either of you ever need it."

Jennifer liked the idea. Christopher's thoughtfulness made her feel safer. It also made her a little sad, for he must have understood that she still didn't fully trust him to be there if she closed her eyes for a moment too long.

"Thank you," she whispered. "That's very generous of you."

"Better hold that praise for after a few weeks' work, woman. I promise, you'll earn every penny."

But hard work didn't faze Jennifer. She loved living and working at Donan. The gardens lay in neglect, but here and there she found the still-living rootstock of an ancient rosebush gone wild or the remains of an herb garden from whose abundance an eighteenth-century cook had plucked thyme, sweet basil, marjoram, rosemary and lavender.

She loved walking the property. There were stables, grooms' and groundskeepers' quarters and the Clarks' cottage. And everywhere were the ruins of stone huts and sheds. The property must have supported a small village at one time.

The days were long, yet there was always more to do than time allowed. Rebuilding a fallen-down stone wall around the west gardens. Patching plaster along the far end of the first-floor hallway. Stripping and refinishing wood trim in a small but elegant salon that once might have belonged to a mistress of Donan.

But they sometimes took time out for a leisurely horseback ride across the moor. And at the end of every day, there was a delicious dinner prepared by Mrs. Clark and a long, lazy sit by the fire over glasses of fruity local wine. Jennifer couldn't have been happier.

Two weeks after she had come to Castle Donan, Christopher announced he would need to take a half day off to deal with business at Lisa's school. "You wouldn't want to play hooky for the afternoon and come with me, would you?" he asked.

Jennifer couldn't resist a drive through the Borders with the man she was growing to love more every day. For it *was* love—she was sure of it now. A love she'd only dreamed of, never believing she would find it for herself. The weather promised to be mild and sunny, once the early mists burned off. They traveled at a leisurely pace, considering the driver's usual preference for speed.

"That's the second abbey we've passed in less than ten miles," she commented. The ruins were marked on the map she'd been using to follow their route. The cold gray stone turned green or black with lichen and moss and the ravages of the weather.

"Both destroyed by Henry VIII in 1544 when he invaded Scotland. Mary, Queen of Scots, was just a young child then."

How hauntingly sad they looked...but proud and beautiful still. Jennifer gazed across the purring car at Christopher. He was a man of deep sensibilities and a belief in honor. Two reasons for his wanting to restore Castle Donan and offer her to the people. Two more reasons for admiring him, she thought blissfully.

St. James rose up out of the flat land to the right of the highway. Plantings of heather and evergreen shrubs softened the stone facades of the buildings. Christopher parked in a space in front of the administrative office.

"I have to pick up some paperwork. The budget and bids for new buildings. Stroll around the campus if you like. I'll catch up with you in a few minutes."

Jennifer walked away from the Jaguar, inhaling the sweet country air. The campus was a cluster of stone buildings—a large one for the administration, three more for classrooms. The remaining structures were cottages, also of stone, and were named for local villages or historical sites—Drumlanrig's Tower, Common Riding, Abbotsford, Dryburgh. Cozy dormitories for the girls, she suspected.

Beyond the last cottage was a gravel walkway and beyond that an athletic field. She could see a group of about twenty young girls, scrambling after a ball, swinging sticks at it, usually but not always missing one another. At last their instructor whistled them all to order, and they formed a tidy double line to march back to the school.

Christopher came up behind Jennifer and stood with his arms around her. "Remembering your girlhood days?"

"They look as if they're having such fun."

"St. James is a good school. I'm glad Lisa is here."

She looked up at his wistful tone. A deep sadness etched fine lines around his expressive eyes and mouth. When she turned back again, the column of chattering girls was drawing closer. Jennifer looked down the ranks and hit on a pair of Parrish-blue eyes. As riveting as the blue eyes of the man standing beside her. She pulled in a sharp breath.

"That's Lisa, right?" she whispered.

Christopher stood silently. She looked up and he was staring intently at the little girl. "We'd better leave," he said, and turned toward the car.

"Wait. Please, Chris. I'd love to meet her."

"That's impossible," he snapped.

"Why?" He was dragging her along after him. "Chris, you said you're a friend of the family. She knows you and—"

"No!" he growled.

Her mouth felt suddenly dry. A spot on her temple throbbed uncomfortably. Why didn't he want her to meet his daughter?

But she didn't have time to dwell on the question, because a high-pitched squeal split the morning air. "Uncle Chris! Uncle Chris!"

The earl came to a sudden stop. An adorable pony-tailed child caught up with them. She threw herself at Christopher, hugging him warmly.

"You came to see me! How very, very nice...and who is your friend?" she asked, sounding far too mature for her years. She turned to Jennifer. "I'm Lisa Ellington. Are you Uncle Chris's new lady friend?"

Jennifer blinked at the little girl's candidness. Apparently, it wasn't the first time Lisa had seen Christopher accompanied by a woman.

"This is Jennifer," he said quickly. "She's visiting from the United States."

Jennifer winced. *Visiting.* Is that all it was?

"Hello, Miss Jennifer," Lisa said brightly. Her instructor had kept the line marching toward the buildings, and now called out to Lisa, but the child ignored her. "You're very pretty. Are you staying at the castle?"

"Yes." Jennifer smiled. "I am. It's beautiful, don't you think?"

Lisa wrinkled her nose. "The rooms smell bad."

Jennifer laughed, enchanted. "That's because they're very old. We're working on fixing them up. They won't smell bad when we're done."

"Good." Lisa turned to Christopher. "Look at my new shoes. Aren't they beautiful? For athletic shoes, that is."

Christopher looked a little less uncomfortable, as if he was beginning to feel everything would be all right. "Very sporty. Where did you get them?"

"My father bought them for me in Paris. We went together, you know. Mama, Papa and I. It was a jolly holiday. We went shopping every day." She looked up at him sheepishly. "I wanted to bring you back a present, the way you do for me sometimes. But Mama said it wasn't ap-ap-appropriate."

Jennifer watched sadly as Christopher's smile stiffened. She felt terrible for him. How awful to hear another man called the father of *his* child.

"Don't worry about it," he said slowly. "You'd better run along before your group leaves you behind."

The little girl glanced worriedly over her shoulder. She started running after the girls at the end of the line. "Come to the house for a visit, Uncle Chris! Please, please do…"

"I will," he said with all the cheerfulness of a log.

Jennifer squeezed his arm. "I'm so sorry. I hadn't realized how difficult it must be for you."

He shrugged. "She didn't mean anything by it."

"Of course not. She just doesn't know. Why not tell her the truth?"

He shook his head. "That's up to her mother. We agreed. When Lisa is old enough."

A skeptical chill swept across Jennifer's mind. "She seems old and bright enough to understand now. You're miserable, and the two of you should have more time together. Before long she'll be a teenager, then a young woman. You'll have missed being the father to her that—"

"I know!" he shouted, glaring at her.

She released his arm and took a step back. The anger in his eyes was new to her and terrifying. "I'm sorry…I didn't mean—"

"Don't you think I feel the passing of every day?" he growled. "Don't you think I *want* to have Lisa with me?"

Jennifer's eyes filled with tears. She was trembling, but not out of fear. Compassion was the only emotion she felt. She faced up to his rage. "Of course, but you have to keep on fighting—don't you see? There must be something that—"

"There's nothing I can do, damn it! It's gone on too long…this stupid lie." He glared off into the distance. "Lisa trusts me. I'm her friend, her Uncle Chris. Telling her the truth would be admitting I've lied to her all these years."

Jennifer shook her head, wanting to offer him comfort, but unable to find words.

"Who knows," he groaned, "she might not even believe me."

"What about her mother? Wouldn't she back you up, if Lisa asked about you?"

"I'm not sure," he said thrusting shaking fingers through his short, dark hair. His face was still flushed with anger, and his voice sounded drained of its usual energy. "I don't think Sandra wants her friends to know Lisa isn't her husband's child. At one time she might have believed it would be all right. But now—" He sighed.

"Please, Chris—for Lisa's sake if not your own—"

"I don't want to talk about it," he said shortly. "It's none of your business, anyway." Abruptly he spun away and strode toward the parking lot.

Jennifer felt as if she'd been slapped across the face.

So this was where Christopher drew the line. His daughter, father, brothers and his brother's wife and children were all family. They might not see each other for months, or even years at a time. But *they were family.* His American girlfriend was temporary…outside of that special circle. And he meant to keep her that way.

Eight

Jennifer spent all of the next day in the garden on the west side of the castle. While she revived ancient rosebushes and dug holes to plant newly purchased varieties, Christopher labored silently on the crumbled stone wall down the hill toward the loch. Mr. Clark had told her that the wall probably had lain in ruins since the last siege of Castle Donan, but Christopher was determined that it should be rebuilt.

Although he was bare-chested and the autumn air was chilly, sweat trickled down the deep crease in the center of his back and over the muscled ridges of his chest and stomach. They spoke only a few words to each other all morning. Jennifer could feel a chasm widening between them.

By late afternoon she was so tired she could barely stand. Every pore of her body felt plugged with Borders' soil, and her heart was heavy. She had tried, off and on throughout the day, to connect with Christopher, but he had removed himself to a world of his own torment.

At dinner that night the silence continued. Jennifer sighed audibly, put down her fork and looked across the table at Christopher. ''You should speak to her mother.''

He cut into the lamb roast on his plate, took a bite and chewed. His jaw tightened and mechanically ground at the meat, and he didn't look up at her.

''Chris, you can't go on like this. By all rights, Lisa should be with you for half of every year.'' Jennifer's voice trembled with emotion. ''You've done nothing to deserve this treatment.''

The anger he'd held on to only by threads during the day, shot to the surface. ''You're right!'' he barked. ''But I told you, nothing's to be done.''

She ignored the cold fire in his eyes and plunged on. ''There *is* something. Lisa is a bright young girl, and she obviously feels very close to you already. I don't believe she would hold it against you for not telling her you are her father. She just needs help understanding the reasons the truth has been kept from her until now.''

''That's not what her mother thinks.''

Jennifer shook her head. ''The woman clearly has her own agenda. She's not concerned with her daughter's welfare, or yours. Maybe she just doesn't want to rock her social boat. Does her husband know?''

''Of course he knows!'' Why was she badgering him? Why wouldn't she leave him to deal with his loss in his own way? ''I wouldn't have agreed to silence if it meant tricking the man into thinking he was Lisa's father.''

"Then something else is going on that we don't know about. The point is, you can't let her keep Lisa to herself this way. It's destroying you."

"I believe it's up to me to decide what I can or cannot tolerate," he growled.

She glared at him, her eyes afire. "That's macho baloney. Men think they can suffer through anything."

"I have so far," he stated. So what if she was right about his being entitled to Lisa. What was the point?

"Please, Chris, talk to the woman. I'll go with you, if you like. Maybe seeing that you have someone permanent in your life will make a difference."

"I doubt it." But then he paused before finally admitting, "I suppose we might try."

The Ellingtons' town house in London was an immense four-story affair in a chic part of the city. Despite her assurances to Christopher that she wanted to go with him, Jennifer fidgeted in the car all the way to the city and felt sick with nerves. She sensed how much depended upon this meeting with the Ellingtons. But Christopher's handsome face remained empty of emotion for the entire drive.

The Ellingtons' door was answered by a butler, who ushered them into an intimate sitting room where a fire blazed behind an ornate screen. The furnishings were light and feminine, the decor ornate with gold filigree and gilded frames around oil portraits of pompous-looking men and women, some in powdered white wigs.

The distinguished ancestors, Jennifer thought, trying not to smile at the thought of some of the rogues she and her mother could have displayed in their own living rooms.

Before Jennifer could say anything to Christopher about the paintings, the door opened and in stepped a handsome woman dressed in a turquoise silk suit. Jennifer could immediately see why men would be drawn to her. Although not really pretty, she exuded a sophisticated sensuality, which was undiminished by the present look of displeasure on her face.

"Please, sit down, both of you. How have you been, Christopher?" she asked stiffly.

"Well. And you, Sandra?"

She nodded, perched on a brocade chair and looked pointedly at Jennifer.

"This is Jennifer Murphy," Christopher said. "She's helping me with restorations at Donan."

Again, not a word that would indicate she was anything more to him than an employee. Jennifer tried to ignore the tiny cold prick at her heart, but it was impossible.

"I see," Sandra said. "Then you have a massive job ahead of you, my dear. The last time I was at Donan, little more than half the castle was in livable condition."

Christopher didn't give Jennifer a chance to respond. "It's coming along," he said coolly. "Will Sir Isaac be able to join us?"

"He's very sorry not to be here," she said quickly. "But we can talk, the three of us. You said this meeting had something to do with my daughter?"

"With Lisa...*our daughter*," he stated emphatically. "She will be seven years old next month."

"I am aware of her age." Sandra shot an annoyed look at Jennifer as if upset that she knew their secret.

Jennifer spoke up. "It would seem that Lisa's old enough to learn who her father is."

The woman's face hardened, losing all of its attractiveness.

"What a foolish thing to say. Of course a young child can't understand that the man she's always known as her father, isn't. And what do you think that would do to the way she's treated at school? Everyone will know she is a *bastard*."

The muscles in Christopher's face contorted. "People aren't that closed-minded these days. Many children are born out of wedlock or have stepparents."

"*Not* in *my* family," she said distinctly. "I refuse to embarrass my husband by causing a scandal at this late date."

Christopher glared at her. "You promised, Sandra. Now you're saying that it doesn't matter how old she is!"

"It's in the child's best interest."

Jennifer stared at the woman's impassive expression. It was clear she believed that she held all the cards and could do anything she wished. She didn't care that Christopher was in pain or her daughter would miss out on a wonderful relationship with her real father.

"This is totally unfair!" Jennifer blurted out.

Christopher gave her a look meant to silence her.

"Fair or not, it's the way it will be," Sandra stated. "And if you, Lord Smythe, dare to tell my daughter that anyone other than Sir Isaac is her father, I will deny it. You won't be welcome in this house, and Lisa will be instructed never to speak to you again."

Christopher bolted to his feet, outrage flaming in his features. "You wouldn't!"

"I most certainly would." Sandra looked pleased with herself. "Perhaps at one time it didn't seem so terrible to admit I'd had affairs before I married Sir Isaac. But he's running for the House of Commons, you know, and that will mean more than the usual emphasis on propriety. We won't be the object of gossip."

Jennifer started to object again, but when she looked at Christopher, she could see that he had already accepted defeat. When Christopher moved toward the door to leave, Jennifer followed behind him, sharing his agony.

The butler was waiting outside the sitting room. He escorted them to the front door. As they passed through it, a gray-haired, stately looking gentleman came up the stone steps.

"Smythe," the man said shortly, nodding at Christopher.

"Good morning, sir," Christopher returned with equal reserve.

They were in the car before Jennifer asked, "Who was that going in as we left?"

"Sir Isaac, Sandra's husband."

"I thought he was tied up for the day."

Christopher shrugged. What did it matter? "Perhaps he chose not to be part of the discussion. He must have thought we had already left."

"I'm sorry it didn't turn out better," Jennifer whispered.

Christopher laid a hand on her knee as he pulled into traffic, glad that she had been with him on this most disappointing of days. Her presence made him feel less empty inside.

"I didn't expect it to be that bad," he murmured. "Sandra has never been this unreasonable."

Jennifer nodded, tenderly touched his hand, then cushioned it between her own. "She definitely has you in a pinch. Do you think she'd really make good on her threat?"

"In a heartbeat."

She sighed. "I don't know anything about the British legal system, but in the United States if she denied you visiting rights with Lisa, you could take her to court. Even if you just threatened to do something like that, wouldn't she give in? She certainly wouldn't want a lot of publicity in the middle of Sir Isaac's bid for a seat in Parliament."

He appreciated her support. But things weren't as clear-cut as Jennifer saw them. "I'm not sure I'd dare call Sandra's bluff. What if she decided to fight me? The British press would smell a scandal. Lisa would be caught in the middle. I can't put her through that."

"No," Jennifer said sadly, "of course not."

But as they drove north again, Christopher thought that confronting Sandra might not have been the worst thing. At least he'd acted. At Jennifer's urging, he had *done* something instead of brooding helplessly. He felt better for it, at least for the time being.

That night as they lay together in bed, Christopher kissed Jennifer good-night on the tip of her nose, their signal that they wouldn't make love that night but that all was well between them. However, Jennifer took things into her own increasingly capable hands.

Lifting the sheet, she slid down beneath the covers.

"What's this all about?" he asked with a surprised laugh.

She pressed her lips to his bare stomach and smoothed her hands upward over his muscled chest. "It's been a nasty day. You need to relax, m'lord," she purred playfully.

"What makes you think I'm not— Good grief! What are you doing, Jenny?"

She trailed kisses down the patch of male fur below his navel, lower still, then pressed her cheek over him. He hardened beneath the soft pad of her cheek.

Christopher groaned. "Getting a little adventurous, aren't you?"

"I'm experimenting. Are you game?"

"Be my guest." He chuckled, delighted with her spirit.

She closed one hand around him, touched him tentatively with the tip of her tongue, stroked him and closed her lips around him. Christopher moaned with each subtle motion of her mouth and loving fingers before he clutched her fiercely to him. A low primal moan of male satisfaction escaped his lips.

Five days of black skies, unrelenting rain and no opportunity to work out-of-doors inevitably darkened Christopher's mood again.

Jennifer kept herself busy. She surveyed the furnishings of the bedroom where she was refinishing the crown molding—a jumble of lovely eighteenth-century antiques, flea-market junk, two marble-topped tables that might be as old as the castle itself and a moth-eaten fifties recliner. With the help of two stable hands she carted away the furniture that was of no value, then rearranged the room with the period pieces alone.

Christopher poked his head inside and looked

around. "They told me you were throwing out perfectly good stuff."

"Perfectly good for a rummage sale," she declared. "Displaying cheap modern furniture alongside such gorgeous old things is a crime. It's fine to mix centuries and styles, as long as each piece lives up to Donan's traditions."

"The room still needs a bed," Christopher commented thoughtfully.

"When the weather clears, I'll visit a couple of nearby estate sales," she said. "In the meantime, we can go through the other rooms and choose what to keep or give away."

Jennifer worked energetically, enjoying the challenge of identifying rare treasures from Donan's forgotten rooms with the help of catalogs ordered from the museum in Edinburgh.

Christopher strove to show enthusiasm for her efforts, but she often found him wandering the castle halls, doing battle with a dour mood. When he tried to help her, his mind drifted and he accomplished little. She feared that all of her cheerfulness and hard work were doing him little good.

One day his old spirit unexpectedly reappeared. He announced that the weather was predicted to clear in the afternoon, and they would drive to a friend's estate where there was to be a polo match. He assured her that this group was friendly and would welcome her.

The grooms loaded their boss's four favorite horses into a trailer, since frequent changes of mounts were required in a hard-ridden game of polo. The trailer was hitched to a truck and driven by the head groom, Jamie. Jennifer rode with Christopher in the Jaguar.

He talked nonstop all the way. Jennifer was thrilled to see the change, but wary, too, for the sudden shift in moods was unsettling.

"I'll ride Prince's Pride first," he told Jamie when they arrived at the host estate. "It may be a few hours before we begin, but you might as well get him ready."

A crowd of cars, horse vans, riders and observers rapidly gathered around the edges of the broad field that stretched below an elegant country house. Under a pavilion warmed by a toasty fire, an elaborate spread of food awaited hungry guests. Christopher introduced Jennifer to everyone. Many people had heard that Castle Donan was in the throes of a major restoration and everyone was eager for details.

"Jenny is amazing." Christopher smiled appreciatively at her and squeezed her hand. "She has an excellent historical background and makes all the right decisions."

"I would love you to have a peek at a few of my rooms," their hostess said with a hopeful smile. "Is it your business, restoration?"

"No," Jennifer admitted, "but I wouldn't mind if it were. I'm enjoying myself immensely."

"Well, let's have a look-see," the woman said and gave Christopher a knowing wink. "If Lord Smythe can spare you?"

He kissed her heartily on the mouth and gave her an encouraging nudge. "Off you go, then. I'll stay with the horses."

The peek at a few rooms turned out to be an hour-long excursion of the Victorian mansion. But Jennifer so enjoyed herself time didn't matter. She was able to give Emma Dorchester several ideas for redecorating. And while they talked about furnishings, wall-paper, paint and historical details of the house, Jennifer learned more about Emma. All of which she liked. Married to a diamond importer, she was a granddaughter of a famous prime minister of England. Emma loved her extensive gardens and worked often in them, but her favorite hobby was jewelry design. Her creations were in high demand in exclusive London shops.

They ended up in front of a window overlooking the polo field. Riders were mounted and taking practice swats with long-handled mallets at small balls hidden by the grass.

"Oh, they're starting already," Jennifer cried excitedly. This time she would be pulling for Christopher, not wishing for his demise.

"So they are." Emma took her arm. "Let's go down. I thought we'd wait a little longer but someone must be eager."

Chris, Jennifer thought immediately.

She could see him tearing up and down the field on the glistening back of Prince's Pride. The black horse dug in its hooves as it spun in a sharp turn at the tug on his reins, sending clods of turf flying.

This is why we're here, she realized.

For a few hours Christopher would try to wipe from his mind the bitter disappointment that plagued him. Visions of the tragic riding accident of a famous actor flashed through her mind. Jennifer felt the need to keep a close watch on him.

"Yes, let's go," she said breathlessly.

Christopher saw Jennifer standing at the far end of the field. He finished negotiating a handicap with the other team's field captain, spun his horse and rode at breakneck pace to pull up with just inches to spare in front of her.

He felt stronger than he had in days. Prince snuffled and flared his nostrils, dancing restlessly beneath him as if just as eager to begin.

"Wish me luck, luv. We've got a lot riding on this match, and I had to give the other side four bloody points!"

"More money for Lisa's school?" she asked.

"This time most will go to a school in Edinburgh for troubled kids."

She smiled up at him and stroked his horse's velvety muzzle. "Fund-raising seems to be developing into a profession for you."

He shrugged. "I like the kids, what can I say?"

"Just be careful out there," she whispered.

He bent down from his saddle and kissed her on the mouth, amused but also warmed by the apprehension in her pretty green eyes.

Wheeling his mount, he left her to find a seat among the folding chairs arranged along one side of the field. He kept Prince moving while the remaining players took the field. Four to each team. The two umpires mounted up. The referee signaled the start of the first period, and they were off.

"Have you ever played?" Jennifer asked Emma when she took the seat beside her.

"Far too many broken bones for my taste. I'd rather watch."

Jennifer followed the play, sliding farther and farther forward on her seat. The speed of the horses, shouts of the players, cracks of mallets and earth-shaking hoofbeats made her feel part of the fierce action.

To her surprise the horses were all Thoroughbreds—big, strong animals topping a thousand pounds each, not the agile polo ponies she had imagined galloping lightly down the field. The first of the six, seven-minute periods came to an end with the score 1-to-2 in favor of the other side.

Christopher had ridden hard and taken far more risks than in the other match she had watched. Several players changed horses, but Christopher did not.

In the second period he played even more recklessly. He ran his horse full-out at the ball, swinging his long-handled mallet like a Scottish warrior attacking the enemy. Standing in his stirrups, he shouted commands to his teammates and traded curses or victorious bellows. High-strung mounts collided, were forced off the line of play, then retaliated by bumping an opponent out of range of a shot. As brutal as the game seemed to her, few fouls were called.

The rich appeared to enjoy playing rough.

At the second break Christopher still didn't bring Prince's Pride to the sidelines. Jennifer noticed Jamie waving at him from the edge of the field, holding the bridle of one of his other horses. Christopher shook him off.

"Damn him," Jennifer muttered. She pushed up from her chair and jogged down the sideline to where the groom stood, looking annoyed. "What's wrong, Jamie?"

"Lord Smythe is like a madman t'day," the older man grumbled. "If he don't change horses soon, he'll be killin' off that handsome animal."

Jennifer's chest tightened as she watched Prince's

Pride stumble through a fast turn. Christopher's eyes were bright and fixed on the ball as he kicked the horse on. Prince snorted, strained, rolled his eyes but plunged on obediently.

Impulsively Jennifer dashed down the edge of the field as close as possible to the tangle of horses and riders engulfed in a cloud of dust.

"Christopher!" she shouted between cupped palms. "Take another horse!"

He flashed her a wild look and kept on riding.

"You'll destroy him if you—" Three horses veered in her direction. She jumped out of their way. Christopher shot her a warning glare. "That arrogant jerk," she swore.

Her heart pounding, Jennifer ran back to Jamie.

"Don't be doin' that, miss," he warned. "It's dangerous standin' out on the field like that."

"Then give me that horse, and I won't be standing," she shouted above the noise of thundering hooves.

He stared at her. "But Lord Smythe will be needin' him in—"

"He needs him *right now,* and he's going to take him if I have to knock him off one damn horse and throw him onto the other."

Without waiting for a response, Jennifer seized the chestnut's reins.

It was fortunate that she had spent time riding between chores at Donan. The second horse was impatient to have his turn at the game. She was barely into the saddle before he broke into a gallop across the field. She didn't even have to steer him in the right direction. His instincts led him directly toward the crowd of horses, milling wildly around the ball.

A whistle shrieked, and shouts from the umpires brought play to a sudden halt. Christopher turned in his saddle with a puzzled glare and finally saw her riding toward him. "What the bloody hell are you—"

"*You,*" she asserted, "are changing horses. *Now,* sir!" She brought the chestnut up close to Prince and slid from her saddle to the ground. Before Christopher could object, she gripped his mount's bridle to prevent him from riding away.

A burst of laughter rose from the dust-covered riders around them.

"Guess she told you, Smythe!"

"We know who's boss at Castle Donan these days!"

Jennifer feared the worst. Christopher had a temper, and his expression at the moment was black and volatile. Stepping closer, she reached up and laid her free hand on his knee as his horse's breath rattled in and out of its heaving chest. Its muzzle was thick with white froth.

"Kill yourself if you like," she whispered urgently at him, "but don't take this loyal creature with you."

Christopher stared at her in disbelief. *No one* ever interrupted play other than the ref or the umpires, and even they sometimes had trouble making themselves heard in a heated game. Jennifer was dwarfed by the ten restless horses and their athletic riders milling around her.

The rage drained from his heart. He was amazed by her nerve. Slowly his mind cleared and he took stock of his mount's condition. The horse's massive ribs expanded and contracted with effort; its forelegs were trembling; its coat streamed sweat. Another ten minutes, and he might have ruined him forever.

"Thank you," he said, his voice gruff with exertion as he pressed a damp palm over her hand and slid off Prince.

They walked the two horses to a table where cold drinks had been set out for the players. Jamie took Prince's Pride away for a good rubdown and rest, and Christopher drank thirstily from a bottle of spring water.

"Don't worry, you'll get your money for the schools," she said, although she knew it was more than charity that drove him to gamble with his life.

Eventually Christopher's team won by a handsome margin, even with their handicap. But he was so exhausted they decided not to stay for Emma's dinner that evening.

"Would you mind driving?" he asked as he pulled off his muddy shirt and riding breeches, using the horse van as a changing room.

She handed him a clean shirt and pants. "I actually get to drive the Jaguar?" she teased. "You must really be tired to trust her to a female driver."

"If I can trust her to anyone, it would be you." He smiled wearily at her. "While you drive, I'll count the spoils."

Fifteen minutes later Jennifer steered the sports car onto the back road leading to Donan.

"How much did we take in?" she asked, feeling like the getaway driver after a bank heist. She could see twenty- and hundred-pound notes, but also a dozen or more checks for amounts that danced with zeroes.

Christopher added up the proceeds silently. "Nearly five thousand."

She gasped. "Five-thousand pounds!"

He laughed. "Should buy those little ruffians some new books and three or four computers for their classrooms, don't you think?"

"That's wonderful," Jennifer said, then turned her attention to the road. He watched her drive for a while, then dozed off in the passenger seat as the adrenaline in his system slowly seeped away. When he opened his eyes, she was slanting a questioning look at him.

"Awake now?" she asked.

"Yup. Good as new." Except when he moved a sharp pain jabbed at his left side, which made him wonder if he might have cracked a rib.

"Great, I have an interesting thought," she said cautiously as she passed a slow-moving lorry. "Why don't I take the train into London someday this week, by myself."

"To buy furniture?" he guessed.

"To have lunch with Lady Ellington."

It felt as if she had driven a blade into his chest. Christopher straightened in the passenger seat but said nothing.

"I'm serious, Chris," she said softly. "I might be able to reason with Sandra if I can just speak to her alone. Woman to woman. She can't possibly understand how difficult being apart from Lisa has been for—"

"No!" he roared.

Jennifer's fingers tightened on the steering wheel. Her chin tilted defensively upward. "You're impossible," she huffed. "I understand there's a matter of pride here. But it's foolish to go on like this. There must be a way to mediate the situation."

"Stop the car!" he roared.

They were moving at well over fifty miles an hour, and the shoulder was nonexistent. "No," she said stubbornly.

"Pull over. I'm going to drive."

She pressed down on the accelerator.

"Bloody hell!" he growled, reaching for the steering wheel.

If she refused to steer the car to the side of the road, he would do it from where he sat. He was stronger, and she wouldn't be foolish enough to try to stop him.

"All right!" she cried. "Let go. You'll get us both killed. I'll do it."

As soon as the car rolled to a stop, Christopher threw himself out the Jaguar's door and ran around to the driver's side. He swung open the door and yanked Jennifer out. She had no choice but to walk around and climb into the passenger seat. He could feel her anger with him, and he didn't care.

Christopher drove in silence. Few vehicles were moving fast enough for him. He passed three or four, then found a clear stretch of road.

"You're being unreasonable," she said at last.

"I'm being practical. Anything you do or say to Sandra now will only make the situation worse. I forbid you to approach the woman." He felt her glaring at him, but kept his eyes to the road.

"I don't see how things can be any worse than this," she countered tightly. "You're miserable. Lisa's totally in the dark about her true history, which may someday be very important to her. And everyone around you from the stable boys to Mrs. Clark has to suffer your vile moods."

"Get used to it," he growled.

"I'm not sure that I can," she said heatedly.

He stole a quick glance at her and saw fear mixed with stubbornness. She looked as if she might cry any second...or heave something at him.

Perhaps he had been too harsh, but he had to make her understand how strongly he felt about the risk of losing his daughter. He would make things right with Jennifer later.

Nine

———

Jennifer had never let others make decisions for her. She wasn't about to let Christopher start now.

Besides, she was confident that she could find a way to convince the Ellingtons to tell Lisa about Christopher. A way that would protect Lisa's fragile relationship with Christopher while preventing damage to Sir Isaac's political career and his wife's social standing. Once she worked things out with the Ellingtons, Christopher would realize she had made the right decision for all concerned.

But what if she failed?

What price would she pay for following her instincts over Christopher's wishes? She might lose him and Castle Donan, which she'd grown to love almost as much as the man. Her only consolation then would be knowing she had done all she could for him.

One morning a week after the polo match, Jennifer

remained in bed after Christopher left for his morning ride. A thick gray mist swirled outside the windows. She heard the crunch of his boots as he crossed the gravel drive leading to the stables. He would be gone for several hours.

Jennifer threw off the bedcovers and dressed quickly, but not in her usual work clothes. Twenty minutes later she ran silently down the stone steps to the great hall and dropped a note on the foyer table where the mail was always left. "Gone shopping. Back by supper. Love, J."

She asked one of the stable lads to drive her to the train station, bought her ticket and, later that morning, arrived at Victoria Station. The day before, it had occurred to her that the Ellingtons might not even be in the city, and she had called to be sure. A maid had told her Sir Isaac and his wife would be in residence for the rest of the week. Jennifer hadn't asked for Sandra. She felt sure the woman would refuse to speak to her. All she could do was hope she caught them at home.

She arrived by cab at the Ellingtons' town house in fashionable Chelsea, paid the driver and climbed the marble steps to tap the polished brass door knocker. Jennifer drew a deep breath to calm herself for the coming ordeal. Her hands trembled at her sides, her insides quivered, and she prayed she would find Lisa's mother in a more reasonable mood.

At last footsteps approached from the other side of the door. The same butler opened the door. He cocked a questioning eyebrow at her.

"I wish to speak with Lady Ellington," she said quickly.

"And you are?" he asked.

"Jennifer Murphy, a friend of the earl of Winchester."

A flicker of recognition crossed his dull gray eyes. "Lady Ellington is entertaining luncheon guests. I will tell her you called, Miss Murphy." He started to shut the door.

Hastily Jennifer stepped into the narrow opening. "This is a very important matter. It can't wait," she insisted.

"I doubt that, miss."

To her amazement he tried to force the door shut despite her standing in its way.

She braced her hands on either side of the door and thrust one foot into the foyer. "I'll wait here while you give Lady Ellington a message. Tell her that either she speaks with me now, in private, or I will be joining her party. Then we can all discuss her daughter's future over dessert."

A burst of laughter and clink of silver against china came from the room to their right. Momentarily distracted, the butler turned. By the time he pivoted back, Jennifer had squeezed the rest of the way into the foyer.

"Please leave now, miss. I don't want to have to throw you out."

He took a step forward, but she dodged to one side, then stood her ground.

"If you want to avoid a scene, just give her the message."

What had possessed her? Until this day she would never have dreamed of forcing her way into another person's house. But desperate situations sometimes called for a little insanity. If threats and ultimatums were what it took to bring Christopher and his daughter together, so be it!

With obvious reluctance the man nodded, then stepped around her into the dining room, shutting the door behind him.

Jennifer's heart raced. Her palms were moist with perspiration as she waited anxiously. Soon the latch clicked on the dining room door, and she looked up to see the grim-faced butler followed by the lady of the house.

"What do you think you're doing here?" the woman snapped.

"Our previous conversation was unsatisfactory," Jennifer stated. "You're not treating Christopher Smythe or your daughter fairly. There has to be some kind of compromise."

Sandra glared at her. "This is none of your business. My husband and I are doing what is best for Lisa."

"You broke your promise to Christopher."

Sandra lifted a precisely waxed brow. "Parker, put her out."

Obedient old Parker moved with surprising agility. Before Jennifer could step aside, he had clamped a strong hand around her upper arm and was dragging her toward the front door.

"Stop it!" Jennifer shouted, struggling to free herself. "You have no right to—"

"*What* is going on here?" a voice boomed through the foyer.

Jennifer looked over her shoulder to see the man who had passed her and Chris as they were leaving the Ellingtons' house on their earlier visit. Sir Isaac.

He was ignoring her but looking questioningly at his wife.

"This young woman has forced her way into the house, and Parker is about to eject her." Sandra's eyes blazed. "Why don't you return to our guests, dear. I will be right along."

He turned to observe Jennifer, still trapped in Parker's claw-like grip. "I've seen you before," he said slowly.

"Yes," she gasped, "a few weeks ago. I came with Christopher Smythe to speak with your wife about—" She broke off. Was there a chance he didn't know about the meeting?

"Go on...go on...I was told the meeting was about Lisa. Sandra wanted to offer Lord Smythe a chance to take his daughter for the next school holiday. But as usual the man has no time for the child."

Jennifer's heart leaped into her throat. She glanced quickly at Sandra Ellington's ashen face. A flash of panic crossed the cold gray eyes before the woman deliberately turned away.

Oh my gosh, Jennifer thought. All this time Lisa's stepfather had been led to believe that Christopher wanted nothing to do with raising his little girl.

"Sir Isaac," she began cautiously. "I believe there has been a terrible misunderstanding."

Half an hour later Jennifer finished explaining to Sir Isaac how desperately Christopher had always wanted to be part of his daughter's life. He was silent for a long moment and appeared to be in a state of mild shock.

"Whenever I asked Sandra if we felt we should tell the child about her real father, she said that it wasn't what Smythe wanted,'' Sir Isaac explained, looking embarrassed by his wife's deception. She had returned to her guests at her husband's strong urging, leaving him alone with Jennifer. "Sandra said Christopher preferred to remain free of responsibility, except for his work on the board and the money he contributed to Lisa's education."

"That's not true," Jennifer stated firmly.

"I understand that now. But it all seemed very logical to me at the time. You must be aware of the man's reputation." Sir Isaac's eyes softened, as if he feared hurting her feelings. He appeared to be in his fifties, but his features were vigorous and his eyes shone with intelligence and kindness. "Your earl runs in fast circles, my dear. He and my wife had a very brief affair, before we married. It was unfortunate that it resulted in a pregnancy, but I wouldn't give Lisa up for anything. She is as precious to me as if she were my own." He smiled proudly.

"Maybe, subconsciously, you didn't want to share her," Jennifer suggested.

"Perhaps that was part of my willingness to believe my wife," he admitted. "But had I known that she was lying to me—"

"She might have been trying to protect you from scandal."

An almost boyish laugh burst from Ellington. "I don't give a whit whether people believe Lisa is my daughter or the king of Siam's. When a man has as much money and power as I have, he stops worrying about what other people think." His smile faded, and he folded his hands in his lap, suddenly looking serious again. "But Sandra didn't come from wealth. She's the daughter of working people and has always been sensitive to gossip. I expect that's why she has worked so hard at this deception.''

Jennifer suddenly understood. Sandra Ellington hadn't wanted so much as a whisper of impropriety to mar the perfect aristocratic world she had married into. ''So, what do we do now?''

''I believe we should talk to Lisa. She needs to know what has been kept so long from her. I have no doubt she will find the adjustment relatively easy. She obviously adores Smythe...has since she was a baby.''

Jennifer smiled, her heart soaring with gratitude. ''Thank you. You don't know how much this will mean to Christopher.''

Sir Isaac stood and offered his hand to her. ''Tell Smythe I will be contacting him. And please know that I appreciate your forthrightness, Miss Murphy. You are an admirable woman.''

Noon came and went before Christopher left the stables that day. He had ridden harder and farther than ever before. But his body still felt driven, and his heart still ached with a special kind of loneliness. The sort that only a parent separated from his child can know.

He left his muddy boots in the small tack room off the back of the house and slipped on leather house shoes before entering the kitchen.

''What will we be having for lunch, Mrs. Clark?'' he asked.

''Whatever you like, sir,'' she answered with a sigh, ''it bein' there's only yourself today.''

He stopped and turned to face her. ''What?''

"Miss Murphy has gone shoppin'. Didn't you see her note?"

"No," he mumbled, irritably. "No, I did not."

He had assumed that Jennifer was working on an upstairs chamber. Why hadn't she said anything to him yesterday about a shopping trip? It was thoughtless of her to just take off without giving him any warning.

After a quick sandwich, Christopher went to work again on the stone wall. He considered driving up to St. James to visit Lisa. Maybe bring her some of those special pastel pencils she had told him she needed for her art classes. He had ordered a set for her birthday, but he could always give them to her sooner.

In the end he decided he wouldn't go to the school again so soon. Seeing Lisa gave him a warm paternal feeling while he was with her. But as soon as he left the world turned bleak again. If he didn't have Jennifer in his life, he didn't know what he would do.

The day wore on. At last dusk fell over Loch Kerr and he returned, exhausted and dirty to the house, where Mrs. Clark met him at the back door.

"Miss Murphy just now returned, sir. Said she would be down for a light supper after a change of clothin'."

He nodded. "I'll go up and speak to her. I have to wash up anyway."

If Jennifer was like any other woman, she would have returned loaded down by parcels spilling over with the latest styles. He would be obligated to feign enthusiasm as she modeled each item for him.

He smiled with tired amusement at the thought. All he wanted to do was clean up, get some food into his stomach and fall into bed. But, he supposed, for Jennifer he could pretend excitement over her choices.

Then he would silence her chatter as he did most every night, taking her in his arms and driving all the sadness from his life by making love to her.

Jennifer couldn't wait to tell Christopher the good news.

Tossing her purse and parcels on the bed, she undressed and dashed for the shower. Her skin prickled with anticipation as steamy water trickled down her body, and she hummed happily.

She heard the bedroom door open then close with a solid clack. "Chris, is that you?" she sang out.

"Jenny, is that you?" he teased.

She giggled, rinsing the soap from her body. "Naw. The local burglar has broken in to scrub up before running off with the good silver."

A hand reached behind the shower curtain and groped at air. "Stop that!" she squealed. "I'll be out in a minute."

"No, you won't," his deep voice promised. His shadow shifted on the other side of the curtain.

She didn't have time to wonder what he meant. The plastic liner moved aside, and Christopher stepped under the spray with her. She shuddered at the breathtaking sight of his muscled body, naked under the stream. Rivulets of dusty water ran over the ridges of his body, trickled between darkly curling hairs and down the drain.

"You've been playing in mud again, I see. The garden wall?"

"I made good progress today." He eyed her with undisguised lust and tweaked the brown peak of her nipple between two fingers. His hands on her hips pulled her forward under the spray with him. "Lack of distractions, I suppose." He kissed the tip of her nose.

Jennifer looped her arms up and around his neck and leaned into him. His body felt hard and long and lean against the softness of her breasts and stomach. She closed her eyes and sighed.

The night promised to be even better than she had imagined.

"I want you, Jenny." Christopher ground out the words, his eyes flashing blue fire.

She smiled, delighted. "You have me."

"Trouble is, I'm famished. Skipped lunch almost entirely."

She nodded. "Later then. After we've eaten. And I have some exciting news for you."

He quirked a dark eyebrow questioningly at her.

"The shower isn't the place. I'll tell you at the table," she promised.

She dried herself and dressed quickly in a long satin lounging robe Christopher had bought her in London on one of their antiquing trips. The soft-peach hue set off her complexion well, and she loved the way it clung to her body in an uninterrupted flow— warm and cool all at the same time. When she walked, the fabric slid against her skin, reminding her of Christopher's hands on her body.

As soon as they were seated in the dining room, Mrs. Clark brought in the soup— a rich brown broth full of sweet onions and finely shredded vegetables. Jennifer took two mouthfuls before Christopher looked expectantly across the table at her. His eyes twinkled with curiosity.

"So what is this fabulous news of yours?"

She had relished this moment all the way home to Donan on the train. "It's about Lisa."

He frowned and put down his spoon. "I thought you went shopping. You saw Lisa?"

"No." Jennifer leaned over the table, not wanting to miss his expression when she told him the news. "I went to visit Sandra. I know you said it wouldn't be a good idea, and at first it seemed as if I wasn't going to be able to put even a foot in the door. But I made it clear I wouldn't leave until she heard me out...then Sir Isaac showed up and—"

"What!" The roar from across the table shocked her into silence. "What the bloody hell have you done, woman?"

"I...I just wanted to reason with the woman," she stammered. Perhaps she'd tackled this conversation from the wrong direction, considering Christopher's temper and lack of patience with involved explanations. "I *knew* that there must be a reason why—"

Christopher stood up so abruptly his chair fell over with a clatter. He glared at her.

"You had no right to meddle in my affairs. I told you not to try to see Sandra." He threw his linen napkin down on the table. "Now you've made it all worse."

"But I *haven't!*" she objected, tears of frustration pooling in her eyes. "Listen to me, Christopher. It's going to be all right now. Sir Isaac said that—"

"Good Lord, you've dragged that poor man into this, too! Are you mad?"

Something snapped inside of her. *It wasn't fair!*

After all she had given up to be with Christopher. After all she had done to bring him and his daughter together. And he wouldn't even listen to her. Once again, he had drawn the uncrossable line between family and her. Lisa was his daughter. He loved her, and he had no difficulty saying so. But never in the wild heat of their passion or quiet shared moments of the day had he said those precious words to Jennifer.

Christopher raged at her, but the words no longer penetrated her disappointment. Jennifer gazed numbly across the table at him, hot tears of despair blurring her vision. She could have forced him to listen to her, but her pride simply wouldn't allow it.

"Get out," he growled at her.

She stood shakily at the table. "I couldn't eat now anyway," she whispered.

"I'm not talking about leaving the dining room. I want you out of my house. You've betrayed me."

"I didn't!" she shouted. "How can you be so bull-headed."

"Go!" he commanded coldly.

No matter how much she loved him, she couldn't allow any man to treat her so callously.

"If you don't trust me with this, we never had a chance together," she murmured dully. "You don't have to tell me to leave. I wouldn't stay now under any condition."

She faced him, her chin high, her eyes snapping with defiance and the traces of dignity she'd managed to hold on to.

"I'll leave early in the morning. One of the stable boys will take me to the station. You needn't bother showing up for a polite send-off."

Ten

"At least you did what you could for the man," Evelyn said after Jennifer had blurted out an abbreviated explanation of their breakup. One look at Jennifer's face as she'd walked into Murphy's Worldwide Escapes and Evelyn hadn't even asked for an explanation. She'd just crossed the office, enveloped her daughter in her arms and wept with her. "Someday he will realize what you've given him. And what he's lost by letting you go. Love is like that sometimes. You can give all that you have, but if it isn't returned...you just have to go on."

"The jerk," Jennifer sputtered.

Her mother moved her away just enough to smile at her. "That's better. A few hearty cuss words might be in order, too."

But swearing or name calling wouldn't help, Jennifer knew. Neither would tears. She drew a finger beneath each eye, wiping away the tears and promising herself a whole heart again, someday.

"What do you suppose your arrogant earl will do when he learns the result of your mission?" Evelyn asked.

"If you're thinking he'll rush across the Atlantic to come for me, forget it. All Christopher ever really wanted was his daughter," Jennifer said sadly.

Her mother raised a questioning brow.

"Don't get me wrong, I'm not jealous of Lisa. She's a sweet little girl. The two of them will get along famously. Lisa worships him; anyone can see that." Jennifer shrugged. "I think I was a temporary distraction, something to keep his mind off his problems. Now that he has what he's been searching for, I won't be needed."

"You really believe that?"

"With all my soul," Jennifer whispered.

The backs of her eyelids tickled, but she refused to let fresh tears fall. Enough was enough. Her mother was right, it was time to move on.

"Now," she said, looking around the little office, "it looks as if we could use a few new posters on these walls. Something tropical and sunny—Jamaica, Bermuda, Cancún!"

"Jennifer," her mother said with concern.

She produced a nearly convincing smile and squeezed Evelyn's outstretched hand. "I'll be fine. Really. Just give me a little time."

The days following Jennifer's sudden departure from Castle Donan and Scotland were among the bleakest in the life of the earl of Winchester. Women had drifted into and out of his life over the years.

Occasionally there had been a twinge of regret for the loss of a pleasant companion. But it had never been like this.

Christopher found himself riding for aimless hours. Jamie took to having Prince's Pride saddled and ready at first light.

Christopher could no longer sleep in his own bed because *she* had shared it with him. Jennifer's scent lingered in the linens even after they had been laundered. When exhaustion overtook him, he napped thinly in a leather armchair in his library as the fire burned low in the hearth. He avoided eating in the dining room because her empty chair haunted him. Quick, informal meals in the kitchen with Mrs. Clark and her husband, who also worked for him, became his habit, when he ate at all.

Work on the garden wall stopped. He put off hiring someone to pick up where Jennifer had left off on the upper-floor restorations. For days he didn't open his mail, and the telephone messages, neatly annotated in the book beside the hall phone, weren't answered because he never bothered to read them.

At last Mrs. Clark took him aside. "If you'll pardon me for interferin', sir, someone ought to respond to the post and the calls comin' in daily. There might be somethin' of importance."

Whatever had been important in his life was gone. His sweet daughter. The love of an American woman with a laugh that brought joy to his heart. They were beyond his reach, now and forever. Why should he care about mundane matters like electric bills, invitations to fox hunts or furniture orders?

"Sir?" Mrs. Clark tapped her foot impatiently.

"Take care of them for me, will you?"

"No, sir, I won't!" she retorted sharply.

His head snapped up at her unexpected reaction. He'd known her since childhood, and she'd never spent a cross word on him. "What?"

"I can't be doin' all that, *and* keep up with the work around this house, too! Lord Smythe, you are old enough to run your own life."

He couldn't help grinning at that. She sounded like the cook of his youth, gently chiding him for snitching a sweet before meal.

Then he thought, *Old enough, yes. But wise enough?* It seemed he was not.

"I apologize for expecting too much of you," he said, patting her arm. "Of course I'll handle the mail…and the calls. Just tell me, if you can, what seems the most crucial to respond to first. Any emergencies?"

"I can't say about emergencies, but your brother in America called two days ago, and Sir Isaac has sent you a letter."

"Bloody hell," he mumbled.

It was a rare thing to hear from Matthew, but he always enjoyed news of his latest escapades. The middle brother of the family had built for himself a successful import business in the United States. Although they saw each other only once or twice a year, they spoke on the phone every month or so. He hated to have missed Matt's call, especially at a time like this when he needed cheering up. Perhaps he would call him back later.

As to Sir Isaac, he dreaded the obligatory conversation following Jennifer's invasion of the man's house. Apologies would have to be made, offended sensibilities mended.

Christopher scooped up the mail and telephone log from the hall table and took them along with him into his library. From his desk he punched in the international code for the U.S. then Matt's number…and waited while the phone rang. The answering machine picked up. Christopher left a brief message.

He must now read what Sir Isaac had to say, regardless of how humiliating and painful the words. He could only hope Ellington hadn't completely retracted his open-door policy to his seeing Lisa.

Christopher sliced open the pearl-gray envelope with the silver opener Lisa had given him for Christmas the year before. He read the letter all the way through once, then a second time before its meaning became clear to him.

A lump of emotion closed off his throat, and he felt as if he was choking. Choking over the impossible joy bubbling up through him as the significance of Sir Isaac's words finally sank in.

Lisa was his!

They were going to meet, the four of them—the Ellingtons, Lisa and himself. His daughter would be told the truth, and know that he was her father. Arrangements would be made for Lisa to live with him for generous portions of each year. It was all there in the letter—all he had ever prayed for and more.

Just as quickly as happiness had engulfed him, it was tainted by shame. This, he now realized, had been Jennifer's parting gift to him. She had given him his daughter, probably knowing that she was risking losing him by going to Sandra against his wishes. He had rejected the woman who had sacrificed her happiness for his.

How had he not seen what she was doing? If only he hadn't been so quick to condemn.

Christopher dropped his head into his hands, consumed by his loss. "Jenny," he murmured. "Oh, Jenny, I'm so sorry…"

It was a few days after that when an unexpected visitor arrived at Donan. Christopher had just come back from one of his fierce gallops across the moor and saw the sleek black sedan parked in the drive. He left his horse to Jamie and strode quickly around the house to find his other and older brother, Thomas, observing the half-completed garden wall.

"It's coming along, isn't it?" Thomas Smythe commented matter-of-factly. Their conversations always started this way, as if continuing a discussion started only minutes earlier—even though it was often many months between their visits.

"It was," Christopher said, letting his eyes touch the rocks he had lifted into place as Jennifer stood by his side, directing the process. Her rosebushes were nearby, but he couldn't bear to look at them. He felt his brother's eyes on him and wondered how Thomas knew something was wrong. Thomas always knew, somehow. Maybe it was his training. A king's bodyguard had to see trouble before it happened. But all the way from Elbia?

"I've been in London for a week, vacationing with Diane," Thomas said.

"How is your new bride?" Christopher asked, turning with curiosity to watch the former confirmed bachelor's expression.

"Diane couldn't be better. Nor could I," he said softly and with obvious joy. He was a very big man, and it seemed nothing short of a miracle that a single mother with three kids had gentled him so thoroughly. Marriage, Christopher could see, had done the man a great deal of good.

"So, how is London?" Christopher asked.

"Abuzz with scandalous rumors," Thomas whispered melodramatically. He lifted a thick, black brow, inviting another question.

"Rumors involving whom?"

"You, dear brother. You."

"Oh." So word was out. It hadn't taken long for society to latch on to the news of his paternity. But he had been more or less prepared. And, in the larger scheme of life, it wouldn't matter. The important thing was that he and Lisa could be father and daughter. There would be no more pretending.

"It's not something I'm proud of, Thomas, having a child out of wedlock. But it's best out in the open. Lisa is perfect. I adore her and can't wait for you to meet her."

Thomas studied his expression for a moment longer. "You seem happy enough with the situation. So why do you look as if you've been trampled by a herd of rogue elephants?"

Christopher shrugged. At any other time in his life he would have kept his grief to himself. But this was somehow different. The loss felt too immense for him to carry alone any longer.

"I was seeing a woman...a very special woman." He impatiently blinked away unwanted moisture from his eyes. "Working things out between me and Lisa and Lisa's mother...well, it all became rather intense, and Jennifer got tangled up in it. I treated her very badly. Accused her of—" Christopher swallowed, but his throat still felt too constricted to force words through. He coughed into his hand and avoided his older brother's eyes. "Doesn't matter. The short of it is, I packed her off to America. She didn't deserve to be treated that way. She was the one who arranged for the Ellingtons to let me claim Lisa as my daughter."

"I see," Thomas said. "So on top of being in love with the lady, you owe her a vast personal debt."

"I suppose—" Christopher stared at him. "Love her? Did you say I was in love with her?"

"It definitely sounds that way to me. I've never known you to feel remorse at the departure of any other female who has crossed your path."

"But this was different. *She* was different. I don't think...that is to say, we were great together in a lot of ways, but *love*...I don't know."

Christopher was more than puzzled. He hadn't put a name to his feelings until now, but the need to define them seemed suddenly urgent. He *loved* her? Was that true? He had felt deeply and passionately attached to Jennifer, but love?

However, when Thomas, the man who was newly and intimately acquainted to that mysterious phenomenon, said he'd been in love with Jennifer, he listened and thought very hard about those words.

He had never told her how he felt about her. What if it was true? He shook his head violently.

"Accurately labeling feelings is no longer relevant," he muttered disconsolately. "She's gone. It's too late." Christopher met his brother's eyes, willing him to understand what he himself could not. "She trusted her future to me. I betrayed that trust. Not the other way around, as I accused her."

"You can still try," Thomas said, laying a heavy, but strangely comforting, hand on his brother's shoulder. "You'll regret it if you don't. Believe me, I know. I've been there."

"No," Christopher whispered sadly. "She came back to me once before. This time I went too far. She'll never again believe me."

Evelyn looked up from the university's course catalog she was perusing. "Darling, I love having you work with me. But I think it would be marvelous if you found something for yourself, something you really *love* doing, like restoring old buildings."

Jennifer nodded, letting herself drift back to Castle Donan, Loch Kerr and the vast surrounding moors. "I'll never regret having gone with him, you know. I learned so much in the short time we had together. But as far as restoration is concerned I'll need some formal training to take my instincts beyond the hobby stage."

"Then by all means..." Evelyn handed her daughter the catalog.

Another week passed, and another after that. Chill autumn winds off Chesapeake Bay made a stroll along the harbor less pleasant. Nevertheless, Jennifer continued to walk from her apartment to the travel agency, absorbing a little fresh air and sunshine before beginning her long workday.

During these walks, she remembered Castle Donan vividly. Never would she forget its breathtaking beauty, or the earl of Winchester. He had touched her heart, her body, her soul more intimately and knowingly than any other man ever had or ever could again. Christopher had made her believe in him…in *them*. She wondered if those sorts of feelings came only once in a lifetime.

It was a Friday, and the winter holidays were approaching, so they would be busy. People tended to think more about vacations or finalizing business travel arrangements as the weekend neared. Jennifer let herself into the little shop, out of the cold wind and flipped over the Open sign, although it was still early. She made coffee, but before she could return to her desk, the bell over the door tinkled.

"That you, Mom?" she called out from behind the privacy screen. Their other employee, Jackie, wasn't due in until noon.

There was no answer. She paused and listened.

Footsteps crossed the office floor. A man's, she guessed by their solid weight.

Quickly she set down the can of coffee grounds and stepped out into the main office. He was standing with his back and left shoulder to her so that she first saw him in profile. Jennifer drew a sharp breath at the familiar silhouette and dark, neatly clipped hair.

Chris?

Her heart hammered in her chest.

He turned and smiled at her. "Miss Murphy, is it?"

No. No, it wasn't her Christopher. But her mouth remained dry, and her heart was pounding erratically at the remarkable resemblance. She couldn't move. Couldn't answer him.

"Are you all right, miss?" He took a step forward, frowning in concern at her sudden paralysis.

"I—I'm fine," she stammered. "You just reminded me of someone." Would she always see a little of Christopher in strangers?

But this man...*this man* was no stranger. She *had* seen him somewhere, though she couldn't remember ever having met him. Was it in a photograph at the castle?

Then it struck her. "You're Matthew Smythe!"

"Yes." He smiled again. Her knees wobbled at the memory of another smile that had been just for her. "I was in town. Chris asked that I stop in and inquire about you."

"Inquire?" Her heart leaped in her chest so wildly it was almost painful. She was hearing words, seeing the man, but nothing computed.

"Yes, he wanted to know how you were doing."

"I'm...well, I'm just fine." She straightened her spine and raised her chin in an effort to pull herself together. She even manufactured a brave little smile that she fancied would be good enough to fool him. "And how are the earl and Castle Donan?"

"I understand both are doing well...as well as can be expected without your presence." What had seemed his casual observation of her suddenly became more intense.

Jennifer stiffened under his piercing gaze. "I was *asked* to leave."

"So I've been told. Frankly, seeing you now, I'd have to say my brother was a bloody fool."

She let out a small laugh, acknowledging his flattery. Oh, they were brothers all right. That Smythe charm must run in the family. "It was probably for the best," she said stoically.

"Then you didn't love him?"

She was so shocked by the intimacy of the question she couldn't respond.

At last she forced out the necessary words. "I don't

see that it matters what my feelings were at the time.
It's over.''

"It matters." He stepped forward.

There was that same arrogant, refuse-to-take-no-
for-an-answer spark in Matthew Smythe's eyes that
she'd found so maddening and enticing all at once in
Christopher's. If he was as much like his brother as
she suspected, the man wouldn't leave her office until
he was satisfied with her responses.

"If your brother sent you to investigate the possibility of our getting back together, you can tell him
to forget it!'' she snapped.

"Did you *love* him?" he repeated.

She rolled her eyes and wished for heavenly inter-
vention…or for her mother to step through the door.
Where was the cavalry when you needed it?

He was still watching her. Waiting.

"I *did* love him!" the words burst from her lips.
"Okay? Is that what you wanted to hear? I loved that
exasperating man with all my soul! Are you satisfied?" She knew she was shouting and she didn't
care. "Now please leave."

He didn't move. "Do you *still* love him?"

She glared at him. "*That* is none of your business."

"*Do you still love him?*"

His persistence was unnerving.

"Listen," she said, resigned to the fact that she
wasn't going to get the American branch of the
Smythe family off her property with anything less
than a complete and embarrassingly honest confes-
sion, "I don't suppose I will ever forget or stop loving
that man. But it was clearly a one-sided relationship.
Christopher is incapable of true love for a woman. I

have no doubt he cared about me in his own way. But when he believed I had gone against his wishes, he shut me out of his life.''

She met Matthew's eyes, willing him to understand. ''Let it go. Tell *him* to let it go, too.''

''No.''

Jennifer was sure that the denial had come from the man standing before her. It took another few seconds for her to realize that his lips hadn't moved, and the sound had come from the doorway behind him.

Matthew stepped aside. His younger brother strode into her office. Christopher's eyes were glittering darkly with determination.

Lord, save me from these two, was all she could think. They were ganging up on her.

''You had both better leave,'' she whispered hoarsely. ''Another minute and I swear I'm calling the police.''

''I'll wait outside,'' Matthew offered diplomatically with a wink for his brother. ''Good luck. I expect you'll need it.''

Christopher lifted a hand in silent acknowledgment, but his eyes never moved from Jennifer. ''You were in love with me.''

''Yes,'' she murmured. ''I was.''

''But you didn't say so.''

''Neither did you,'' she countered.

He nodded. ''But I was a fool. You aren't.''

She narrowed her eyes at him. ''I can't go through this again, Chris. Please don't ask me to. You broke my heart.''

''That makes two of us walking around, damaged.'' He took a deep breath. ''Jenny, I loved you from the moment you rumbled up to my castle in that silly red van. I didn't understand that until after you left me. And after I discovered what you had done for me and for Lisa.''

She swallowed, hot tears threatening to spill from behind her eyelashes. ''Then you have her now? You've worked things out with the Ellingtons?''

He nodded slowly. ''Lisa has been told I'm her father. Actually, I think she's most excited about receiving birthday and Christmas presents from two doting dads. She's already spent a few weekends at Donan. The Clarks are thrilled, and I have never been happier.''

''I'm glad,'' she murmured softly. ''I really am, Chris.''

He stepped forward and took her hand in his. ''But I could be even happier.''

''Don't ask me…please don't,'' she pleaded.

''Marry me,'' he said quickly. ''Jennifer, for God's sake, marry me!''

She gasped, shaking her head in disbelief. Perhaps in her wildest dreams she had imagined him coming to her, begging her forgiveness. Dreamed of returning to Donan with him to pick up where they had left off, as lovers and friends. But marriage? She had believed it was the one step he would never take.

''Chris, I…'' She could see past him through the window. Matthew was standing guard, his back to the glass door, blocking the Open sign. Her mother had arrived, and he was chatting her up. Buying his brother time and privacy. ''You don't really mean this.''

''I've never been so serious about anything in my life,'' he said. ''I didn't ask my brother to help me charm a girlfriend back into my bed. I asked him to help me woo my bride. In fact, he insisted I assure him of my honorable intentions before he agreed to approach you." He gently squeezed her fingertips. "I had to hear from your own lips that you loved me. But I was afraid you wouldn't even speak to me if I came on my own behalf."

"You were right," she said shortly.

Christopher seized her shoulders and gave her a gentle shake. "Jenny, don't. Please don't. If you love me and I love you—which I do—we should be together. It can be that simple. But there are other reasons. Castle Donan needs you as its mistress. And Lisa should have a mother even while she's with me, away from Sandra. I can think of no other woman more loving, more sensitive and caring for either job. Come to us. Please."

She could no longer stop the tears. When she had dreamed of returning to Christopher's arms, the images had never been as sweet as this moment.

"Oh, you are a terrible, *terrible* man," she sobbed and fell into his arms. "I love you so."

He kissed her deeply, possessively. In his heart he knew that he would never let her go. From this day forward he would do all any man could to make her happy.

Epilogue

Emma Dorchester insisted on taking charge of the wedding plans the moment the couple returned to England, just a week after Christopher's proposal. "As long as you two are determined to be married in the castle, your mother, Jennifer, will need all the help she can get with arrangements. A busy career woman like Evelyn can't be expected to drop everything and rush off for months to another country."

Emma might be rich, but she was eminently practical. She suggested Christopher delay all renovations at Donan, except for the gardens and the ballroom, where the spring wedding and reception would be held. Then she began arranging for flowers, photographers and extra help in the kitchen to prepare the wedding feast.

"Where will the two of you live?" Emma asked. "At Donan?"

"Part of the year, while Lisa is in school," Jennifer said, remembering the conversation she and Christopher had had only days earlier.

Discussing compromises that would make their life together work smoothly was taking up considerable time at the moment. But she felt confident that they would find ways to handle any of life's hurdles together.

"During the summer months we'll live in Baltimore so that I can help my mom at her busiest time of year. We both like the idea of having two countries to live in."

"So you'll have plenty of time to continue work on Donan," Emma added.

"Yes, the castle means a lot to both of us." But now Jennifer's mind was on the wedding. She was thrilled to have Lady Dorchester's help, and Christopher seemed relieved to leave all the details to the women in his life—Jennifer, Emma, Evelyn and Mrs. Clark. Even Lisa got into the act, offering her services as flower girl.

"I don't think that will do," Jennifer told Christopher's daughter with a shake of her head and a frown.

"Why not?" Lisa cried. "I *want* to be in the wedding!"

Jennifer smiled at her. "Flower girls are usually very little, not much more than babies. You aren't a baby anymore."

"No," Lisa agreed regretfully.

"So I think you should be my bridesmaid. My only bridesmaid."

Lisa looked up at her with glowing azure eyes, so much like her father's. "Really? Really truly?"

"Really truly," Jennifer said, laughing as the little girl threw herself into her arms, hugging her tightly around the neck.

Jennifer looked up to see Christopher walk into the small parlor she had made over into her own office, full of books about decoration and architecture, landscaping and art. "I see you two ladies are getting along." He reached down and scooped up Lisa, swinging her high over his head as she squealed with delight.

"I'm going to be the bridesmaid!"

"Well, that could be dangerous. I don't know."

"It's not dangerous being in a wedding," Lisa giggled.

"Oh, you don't think so? I know quite a few gentlemen who would argue the point."

Jennifer laughed at him and kissed him soundly on the cheek. He put Lisa down, and she ran off to intercept Mrs. Clark who was taking a tray of cookies into the dining room.

Jennifer dropped her arms around his neck and leaned into him playfully. "Does this gentleman think *his* wedding is dangerous?"

Christopher grinned evilly at her. "Absolutely. I'm putting my entire life in your hands, woman. Sounds like risky business to me."

She gently stroked her fingertips across his brow and kissed him softly on the mouth. "That's where trust comes in. Yours in me…mine in you."

The handsome lines of his face smoothed and he observed her solemnly. "I've made my choice. I will never regret it."

"And I've made mine," she said, letting out a contented sigh. "Now, I smell fresh scones and tea brewing. How about it?"

He didn't have to say a word for her to understand that tea would have to wait. The glimmer in his eyes told her what his appetite was set on. Taking her hand, Christopher started out the door and headed for the staircase to the upper floors.

"In the middle of the afternoon?" she asked, pretending shock.

"And every other chance I get," he growled happily. "It's likely, Lady Smythe, that I'll never get enough of you!"

*   *   *   *   *

*Christopher Smythe and his brother Thomas
have happily wed. But can their estranged
brother Matthew ever learn to love?*

*Hurt most deeply by their mother's desertion,
Matt has vowed never to return to England or
trust a woman's tenderness. He has both
wealth and power, but is that enough for the
young entrepreneur dubbed by the press,
the American Earl?*

*Join Lord Matthew Smythe when he meets
the one woman who has a chance of healing
his wounds and winning his heart in
Silhouette Desire's mesmerizing story,*

THE AMERICAN EARL
(February 2001).

January 2001
TALL, DARK & WESTERN
#1339 by Anne Marie Winston

February 2001
THE WAY TO A RANCHER'S HEART
#1345 by Peggy Moreland

March 2001
MILLIONAIRE HUSBAND
#1352 by Leanne Banks
Million-Dollar Men

April 2001
GABRIEL'S GIFT
#1357 by Cait London
Freedom Valley

May 2001
THE TEMPTATION OF
RORY MONAHAN
#1363 by Elizabeth Bevarly

June 2001
A LADY FOR LINCOLN CADE
#1369 by BJ James
Men of Belle Terre

MAN OF THE MONTH

For twenty years Silhouette has been giving
you the ultimate in romantic reads. Come join
the celebration as some of your favorite authors
help celebrate our anniversary with the most
sensual, emotional love stories ever!

Available at your favorite retail outlet.

Where love comes alive™

Visit Silhouette at www.eHarlequin.com   SDMOM01

#1 *New York Times* bestselling author

NORA ROBERTS

brings you more of the loyal and loving, tempestuous and tantalizing Stanislaski family.

Coming in February 2001

The Stanislaski Sisters

Natasha and Rachel

Though raised in the Old World traditions of their family, fiery Natasha Stanislaski and cool, classy Rachel Stanislaski are ready for a *new* world of love....

And also available in February 2001 from Silhouette Special Edition, the newest book in the heartwarming Stanislaski saga

CONSIDERING KATE

Natasha and Spencer Kimball's daughter Kate turns her back on old dreams and returns to her hometown, where she finds the *man* of her dreams.

Available at your favorite retail outlet.

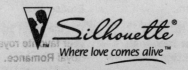

Where love comes alive™

Visit Silhouette at www.eHarlequin.com   PSSTANSIS

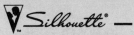

where love comes alive—online...

eHARLEQUIN.com

your romantic books

♥ Shop online! Visit Shop eHarlequin and discover a wide selection of new releases and classic favorites at great discounted prices.

♥ Read our daily and weekly Internet exclusive serials, and participate in our interactive novel in the reading room.

♥ Ever dreamed of being a writer? Enter your chapter for a chance to become a featured author in our Writing Round Robin novel.

• • • • • •

your romantic life

♥ Check out our feature articles on dating, flirting and other important romance topics and get your daily love dose with tips on how to keep the romance alive every day.

• • • • • •

your community

♥ Have a Heart-to-Heart with other members about the latest books and meet your favorite authors.

♥ Discuss your romantic dilemma in the Tales from the Heart message board.

your romantic escapes

♥ Learn what the stars have in store for you with our daily Passionscopes and weekly Erotiscopes.

♥ Get the latest scoop on your favorite royals in Royal Romance.

In March 2001,

Silhouette® Desire®

presents the next book in

DIANA PALMER's

enthralling *Soldiers of Fortune* trilogy:

THE WINTER SOLDIER

Cy Parks had a reputation around Jacobsville for his taciturn and solitary ways. But spirited Lisa Monroe wasn't put off by the mesmerizing mercenary, and drove him to distraction with her sweetly tantalizing kisses. Though he'd never admit it, Cy was getting mighty possessive of the enchanting woman who needed the type of safeguarding only he could provide. But who would protect the beguiling beauty from *him...?*

Soldiers of Fortune...prisoners of love.

Silhouette®
Where love comes alive™

*Available only from
Silhouette Desire at
your favorite retail outlet.*

Visit Silhouette at
www.eHarlequin.com

SDWS

MAITLAND MATERNITY

Where the luckiest babies are born!

In February 2001, look for

FORMULA: FATHER

by Karen Hughes

Bonnie Taylor's biological clock is ticking!

Wary of empty promises and ever finding true love,
the supermodel looks to Mitchell Maitland, the clinic's
fertility specialist, for help in becoming a mother. How can
Mitchell convince Bonnie that behind his lab coats and
test tubes, he is really the perfect man to share her life
and father her children?

*Each book tells a different story about the
world-renowned Maitland Maternity Clinic—
where romances are born, secrets are revealed…
and bundles of joy are delivered.*

Visit us at www.eHarlequin.com   MMCNM-6

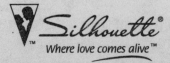